The Darling Buds of May

A Comedy

H. E. Bates

A Samuel French Acting Edition

SAMUEL FRENCH

FOUNDED 1830

SAMUELFRENCH-LONDON.CO.UK
SAMUELFRENCH.COM

FOR AMATEUR PRODUCTION ENQUIRIES

UNITED KINGDOM AND WORLD EXCLUDING NORTH AMERICA

plays@SamuelFrench-London.co.uk

020 7255 4302/01

Each title is subject to availability from Samuel French,

depending upon country of performance.

THE DARLING BUDS OF MAY

The first national tour, on which this acting edition is based, was presented by E & B Productions (Theatre) Ltd and Excelsior Group Productions Ltd, in association with The Royal Theatre, Northampton, and opened at The Royal Theatre, Northampton, on 18th August, 1995 with the following cast of characters:

Pop Larkin	Christopher Timothy
Ma Larkin	Gemma Craven
Mariette	Josie Milton
Montgomery	Alan Horgan
Primrose	Lara Pulver
Petunia	Eloise Delbianco
Zinnia	Helly Orris
Victoria	Charlotte Hall
Mr Charlton (Charley)	Ian Kirkby
Miss Pilchester	Clare Welch
Pauline Jackson	Sarah Louise Mayne
Angela Snow	Satara Lester
The Brigadier	Robert Mill
Sir George Bluff-Gore	Graham Rowe
Lady Bluff-Gore	Sidonie Bond
Tax Inspector	Christopher Mellows

Directed by Alan Cohen
Designed by Ray Lett
Lighting designed by Paul Dennant

Originally presented by Minster Productions Ltd, by arrangement with S.T.P. (Theatres) Ltd, at the Saville Theatre, London, on 2nd September, 1959, with the following cast of characters:

Pop Larkin	Peter Jones
Ma Larkin	Elspeth March
Montgomery	John Symonds
Primrose	Amanda Coxell
Petunia	Delene Scott
Zinnia	Penelope Hamilton-Bell
Victoria	Patricia Wilson
Mariette	Antonia Gilpin
Mr Charlton	John Standing
The Brigadier	Kynaston Reeves
Tax Inspector	Duncan Lewis
Miss Pilchester	Rosamund Greenwood
Pauline Jackson	Claire Gordon
Sir George Bluff-Gore	Tom Macaulay
Lady Bluff-Gore	Audrey Noble
Angela Snow	Jill Melford
Two Ladies	{ Dorothy Baird Rosemary Davies

Directed by Jack Minster
Décor by Timothy O'Brien

CHARACTERS

Pop Larkin
Ma Larkin
Mariette, 17
Montgomery, 15
Primrose, 13 } their children
Petunia, 11
Zinnia, 11
Victoria, 9
Mr Charlton (Charley)
Miss Pilchester
Pauline Jackson
Angela Snow
The Brigadier
Sir George Bluff-Gore
Lady Bluff-Gore
Tax Inspector

SYNOPSIS OF SCENES

The action takes place in the Larkin household, set in luscious woodland countryside in southern England

ACT I
SCENE 1   The Larkin household. May, 1957. Friday afternoon
SCENE 2   The same. Later that evening
SCENE 3   The same. The following Sunday morning

ACT II
SCENE 1   The same. Evening, four days later
SCENE 2   The same. Evening, three weeks later
SCENE 3   The same. Later that evening

Time—1957

One day in 1956, my father handed me the typescript of his latest short story. It was something of a departure, he told me. Something quite different, something ... funny.

I read the story and agreed with him that it was certainly both different and ... funny. Those modest but telling six thousand words were later to become the first chapter of a novel titled *The Darling Buds of May*. A novel that in turn spawned four further novels featuring the indomitable Larkins, a feature film, a radio series, a hugely successful television series and ... a play.

What H. E. Bates created then has stood the test of appreciation by viewers and readers all over the world and I hope that this brand new production of his stage version will be just as warmly received and will give as much pleasure to old and new Larkins' fans alike as it has given us to produce.

Richard Bates
1996

ACT I

The Larkin household, set in luscious woodland countryside in southern England. Four o'clock on a brilliant hot Friday afternoon at the end of May, 1957

The scene is so arranged as to show both the living-room/kitchen of the house and part of the yard outside

The living-room/kitchen presents a monument in fantastic ostentation. An enormous new black and white television set stands in one corner. A vast glass and chromium cocktail cabinet, shaped like a Spanish galleon, fills another. A shining French-polished table stands in the centre. There is also a radio, an impeccable new electric cooker and a large Frigidaire. Chairs, pictures, curtains and other furnishings are of the same lurid standard of extravagance

By contrast, the yard outside is a complete wilderness. Junk of all kinds, old iron, broken pig-troughs, old perambulators, worn-out tyres, sacks, wheels, boxes, corrugated-iron — anything and everything is strewn about in chaotic disorder. Above it all spreads a flowering chestnut tree, in full bloom, on the lower branches of which hang a few worn-out motor-tyres, and behind it all lies the glorious light of the May afternoon

As the CURTAIN *rises the stage is empty. The calls of farm animals and birdsong can be heard in the background. Off stage is heard the sound of a truck drawing up. This is followed by truck doors banging and the joyous laughter of the eight Larkins arriving home, and then by a chorus of disturbed geese, ducks and hens in the background*

The entire Larkin family, with the exception of Mariette, the eldest, now enters the yard weighed down with bags and trays of shopping. Montgomery, the only boy, is fifteen; Primrose is thirteen; Zinnia and Petunia, the twins, are eleven; Victoria, the youngest, is nine. Pop Larkin is fortyish, dark, perky, balding, with side-linings and an air of boisterous, breezy, happy confidence in all he says and does: a likeable, warm-hearted, irrepressible, shrewd, infectious spiv. Ma is two yards wide. She is thirty-seven, dark, well-permed,

*olive-skinned and calm as a bolster. She wears large drop pearl ear-rings as
big as young cherries and several huge turquoise rings on her fingers. Her
vast woollen jumper is salmon. Clearly she was once — and indeed still is —
very handsome. All the Larkins are sucking at the largest chocolate-vanilla-
raspberry ice creams that money can buy. In addition Pop produces half a
dozen packets of potato crisps*

Ma Well, home again, home again, market's done. (*She sits down on an oil-
drum and takes off her shoes, squeezing her tired feet*)
Pop Lovely to be home. Anybody want crisps with their ice-cream?
Montgomery ⎫
Primrose ⎪
Victoria ⎬ (*together*) Please! Please, Pop! Please! Yes, please.
Zinnia ⎪
Petunia ⎭

*Pop, laughing gaily, throws packets of crisps to his starving offspring. The
children catch them and start off for the house. Montgomery opens the door
and lets them in*

Ma Have a good day, Pop?
Pop Oh! fair, Ma, fair. Picked up just over fifty quid on that straw deal.
Another bob or two here and there. Good price for the pigs. And I finally
got rid of those two hundred pairs of Army underpants.
Ma Oh, who to?
Pop The Army, as it happens. Crisps, Ma?
Ma Please. Lovely. Just what I wanted.

*As Pop feels in his pocket for another packet of crisps the children switch on
first the radio, which immediately blares out dance music, and then the
television. All five then sit in front of the screen, hypnotized in its greenish
glow, eating and sucking as hard as they can. At the same time Pop breathes
with ecstasy at the glowing, golden afternoon*

Pop Wonderful day, ain't it? Hark at them blackbirds. Lovely. No it ain't
though. Here, where'd I put that money? Had it when I bought the ice-
creams. Don't say I dropped it. Here, Ma, hold my ice-cream.

*Ma takes Pop's ice-cream. Pop starts a frantic search of his pockets. Ma,
imperturbably, takes a lick first at Pop's ice-cream and then one from her
own*

(*Laughing in his own ringing fashion*) All right, all right. Panic over. Got it mixed up with the crisps. (*He produces a roll of pound notes: about a hundred of them*) Easy to get 'em mixed up. Paper's got the same sort o' crackle.

He puts the money back into his pocket, then produces another packet of crisps. Imperturbably Ma exchanges Pop's ice-cream for the crisps and then goes on sucking and eating

What time is it, Ma?

Ma (*looking at her large and expensive wrist-watch*) Four o'clock.

Pop Just in time for dinner. Want a glass o' beer, Ma? Bar o' chocolate or summat while you're getting dinner? Drop o' cider?

Ma Not just now. I'll have a Guinness when I get the fish and chips warmed up.

Pop Blimey, I'm hungry. Must be the air. Lovely to be home though, Ma, ain't it? Marvellous place we got here. Paradise. Absolute blooming paradise.

Ma Wouldn't change it for nowhere.

Pop Not even for Gore Court?

Ma What, that old place? Court, my foot. Wants pulling down. That's what I'd do with it, pull it down. Only thing for them places. Nobody can keep 'em up.

Pop (*slightly surprised*) True. True. No, we got everything we need. Nice Home. Plenty to eat and drink. Telly. Nice kids we got too.

Ma The best.

Pop By the way, where's Mariette?

Ma About somewhere, I expect. Looking at her horse, I shouldn't wonder.

Pop What she'd do without horses I don't know. Crazy about horses. (*He pauses in the fact of licking his ice-cream, struck by a sudden thought*) Come to think of it, I ain't heard Mariette laughing much recently. What's wrong with her?

Ma I expect she's thinking.

Pop (*stunned*) Thinking?

Ma I got an idea that's what she's been doing.

Pop Thinking? What's she got to think about?

Ma (*licking at her ice-cream, splendidly imperturbable*) She's going to have a baby.

Pop (*also completely unconcerned*) Oh, is she? Jolly good. Nice to have a kid about the place.

Quite undisturbed, Ma and Pop lick at their ice-creams

Whose is it?

Ma She can't make up her mind.
Pop Oh, well. Safety in numbers.
Ma I suppose so.
Pop She'll have to make up her mind some time, won't she?
Ma Why?
Pop Oh. I just thought.
Ma She thinks it's either that Jones boy who worked at the farm, or else that chap who works on the railway line. Harry somebody.
Pop I know him. Nice enough chap.
Ma The other one's overseas now. In the Navy. Far East, or somewhere.
Pop Well, he'll get leave.
Ma Not for a year he won't. And perhaps not then if he hears.
Pop Oh, well, we'll think of something — or somebody. Bound to.
Ma Here's Mariette now. Don't say nothing to her, Pop.

Mariette comes into the yard. She is seventeen: dark, very pretty, with a fine figure that is emphasized by her pale lemon shirt and jodhpurs. She seems perhaps a little quiet and dreamy but otherwise she is not more noticeably worried about anything than Pop and Ma

Pop Hullo, sweetheart. Been to look at the mare?

Mariette makes no answer. She is in fact not even looking at Pop. She is staring past the house, into the farther recesses of the yard

Wonderful day for a ride. Ma, this sun'll soon put some paint on the strawberries. Notice how they were putting the straw on the fields when we came along, Mariette? Soon be strawberry picking now. Best time of the year.

Mariette still makes no answer. She is still staring across the yard

Ma Here, what am I doing standing gossiping? I got dinner to get. The kids must be starving.

She goes into the house, where the kids are still gorging the crisps. Pop approaches Mariette

Pop (*affectionately*) Ah. Come on, Mariette. It's all right. Ma's told me. Nothing to worry about. Nothing to worry about at all.

He is about to put an arm on Mariette's shoulder, but she moves away

Mariette Pop.

Pop Yes? What is it?
Mariette There's a man standing over there in the yard. By the horse-box. He's been there some time.
Pop Man? Blimey, so there is. What's he up to?
Mariette He's coming this way. He's got a briefcase under his arm.
Pop Never seen him before.
Ma (*from the house*) Mariette! Be a duck and slip back to the lorry and bring the pineapples, will you? Three of 'em — in a big basket. Must have 'em for dinner.

Mariette is still watching the man across the yard and again makes no answer

Mariette!
Mariette Yes, Ma. Just going.

Mariette starts to go back to the lorry. At the same time the man, Mr Charlton, appears. As they pass each other he and Mariette pause very briefly. Then Mariette, with her attractive figure swinging a little, goes on. Mr Charlton cannot take his eyes from her and continues to watch her for some seconds longer

Pop Hullo, hullo, hullo. Morning. Afternoon rather. Looking for somebody?

At last Mr Charlton stops staring after Mariette and comes forward. He is about twenty-four, spectacles, pale face, trilby-hat, earnest and rather shy. He carries a black briefcase

Mr Charlton Mr Sidney Larkin?
Pop Larkin, that's me. Larkin by name, Larkin by nature. (*He gives one of his uninhibited, ringing laughs*) What can I do for you. Lovely wevver, 'en it.
Mr Charlton Mr Larkin, I'm from the office of the Inspector of Taxes.

Pop stands blank, stunned and innocent, shocked by the very existence of such a place

Pop Inspector of what?
Mr Charlton Taxes. Inland Revenue.
Pop You must have come to the wrong house.
Mr Charlton You are Mr Sidney Larkin? (*From the briefcase he takes out a form and peers at it*) Sidney Charles Larkin?
Pop That's me. That's me all right.
Mr Charlton Mr Larkin, according to our records you've made no return of income for the past two years.

Pop Return? Return? What return?
Mr Charlton You should have had a form. (*He holds up a buff-yellow form*)
One like this.
Pop Form? Form? I ain't had no form.
Mr Charlton Our records show that several have been sent to you.
Pop (*appealing loudly*) Ma, did we have a form like this? Never had no form,
did we?

*Ma is busy laying the table for dinner. Throughout the following she comes
and goes placing various food, etc. on the table*

Ma Never seen one. Sure we never.
Pop Come over here a minute, Ma. This gentleman's from the Inspector of
Summat or other.
Ma I got dinner to get. (*She moves away*). Everybody's starving. (*She starts
to prepare the meal*)
Pop No. Never had no form. Ma says so.
Mr Charlton You surely must have done. At least three, perhaps four, were
sent to you.
Pop Well, Ma says no. She ought to know. Ma's the one who does all the
paperwork.
Mr Charlton In that case ——

*Mr Charlton is about to hand Pop a fresh form when he is stopped by an
alarming chorus of noise from across the yard*

What on earth was that?
Pop Turkeys. Yelling for their grub. Everybody and everything gets
ravenous in this place. It's the air.
Mr Charlton I see ——
Pop What about a nice hen bird for Christmas? Put your name on it now.
Mr Charlton Mr Larkin — (*very firmly*) — this form must be returned to
the Inspector. There is a statutory obligation ——
Pop Can't return it if I ain't got it, can I?
Mr Charlton That is what I am here for. To see that this time you get it.
Pop Blimey! I got no time for forms. Gawd Almighty, I got pigs to feed,
turkeys to feed, hens to feed, kids to feed. I ain't had no dinner.

Mariette returns with three enormous fresh pineapples in a basket

*Mr Charlton is not listening. He has again become hypnotized by the sight
of Mariette*

(*He stops*) Hullo, what's up? Ah! my eldest daughter. Crazy about horses.

Mad on riding. You do any riding, Mister — Mister — Mister — I never caught your name.

Mr Charlton Charlton.

Pop Mister Charlton, this is Mariette. This gentleman's crazy on horses, Mariette, just like you are. Comes from the Ministry of Revenue or summat.

Mr Charlton (*raising his hat*) How do you do.

Mariette Good-afternoon.

Pop I say every kid should have a horse. I'm going to get every one of my kids a horse.

Mr Charlton Am I mistaken — or did I see you riding in the point-to-point over at Barfield at Easter? You came second.

Mariette That's right.

Pop Hope you won a bob or two on her.

Pop laughs again and further disarms the already confused Mr Charlton by slapping him on the back

Pity we didn't know you were coming, Mr Charlton. We're killing a goose tomorrow. Always kill a goose or a turkey or a few chickens at the weekend. Or guinea fowl. Like guinea fowl?

Ma Dinner's ready! Anybody coming or am I slaving in here for nothing?

Pop We're coming, Ma. Well, got to go, Mr Charlton. Sorry. Ma won't have no waiting.

Mr Charlton Now, Mr Larkin, about this form ——

Mariette Did you see me at Newchurch? I rode there too.

Mr Charlton As a matter of fact, I did, but — Mr Larkin, there is a statutory obligation ——

Pop Sorry, must have my dinner, Mr Charlton. Must have my dinner.

Mariette I tell you what — come and have a bite with us.

Mr Charlton I've eaten, thank you.

Mariette Cup of tea, then. Cup of coffee.

Pop (*frowning at Mariette's invitation*) Mariette ...

Mariette Oh yes, do.

Ma Give it to the cats in two minutes if you're not here!

Mariette I wish I'd known you were at Newchurch. I do wish I'd known.

Pop Come in then, Mr Charlton, come in. We got a beautiful place here. Come on in. Meet the family. Everybody's welcome here.

Against his will, still half-mesmerized, Mr Charlton finds himself in the house, where the kids are now seated, with Ma, at the dinner-table, their faces still bathed in the greenish light of the television set, which they never stop watching

Mariette Sit down, Mr Charlton. Make yourself at home. Anything you don't see, ask for. (*She puts the pineapples on the table*)
Pop Pass the vinegar, Ma.

One by one everybody gets seated at the table, which is now loaded with food of all kinds, including the fish and chips, together with bottles of vinegar, tomato ketchup, Worcester sauce and beer, two big jugs of cream and three large luscious pineapples

Ma Perhaps Mr Charlton would like half a dozen sardines? Monty, fetch the sardines.

Montgomery goes to fetch the sardines

Pop Mr Charlton saw Mariette riding over at Barfield. What's on telly?
Mariette And at Newchurch.
Ma Funny we never saw you there. We was all there.
Pop What is it? Lone Ranger? Mr Charlton's mad on horses, Ma. Just like Mariette.
Ma Turn up the contrast. It's too dark.
Mr Charlton About this form, Mr Larkin. If you've got any difficulties I'd be glad to help you ——
Pop All right: you fill it in.
Ma Still too dark. Turn it up more. It never stops where you want it nowadays.
Pop I'll give the damn thing one more week to behave itself. If it don't then I'll flog it and get another.

Mr Charlton starts to spread the buff-yellow form on the table and unscrews his fountain pen

Mr Charlton Full name: Sidney Charles Larkin ——
Montgomery (*returning with the sardines*) Sardines, Mr Charlton? Help yourself.
Mr Charlton I'm afraid I don't care for sardines.
Ma Ice-cream, then. Have some ice-cream. Primrose, there's a big block o' strawberry mousse in the fridge. Go and get that.
Primrose Yes, Ma. (*She does so*)
Mr Charlton Occupation, Mr Larkin? Dealer?
Ma Don't you call him a dealer. He owns land. We got two lovely meadows at the back. Twenty-five acres. And a wood full of bluebells.
Mr Charlton Very well, landowner ——
Pop Farmer.
Mr Charlton I'm sorry. Occupation: farmer. Now what would you estimate ——

Zinnia
Petunia
Victoria } (*together, excitedly*) Lone Ranger! Lone Ranger!
Montgomery
Primrose

Ma Mariette, cut the pineapple. Have some pineapple, Mr Charlton. And cream. Real cream from our jersey cow.

Mr Charlton I find pineapple too acid, thank you. Mr Larkin, are these all your children?

Pop Blimey, I hope so. Ma, hear that?

Mr Charlton I meant is this all — have you any more?

Pop Well, not yet, old man. Plenty o' time yet though. Give us a chance.

Mr Charlton Six children.

Ma Gone again. Can't see a thing. Montgomery, Primrose — go and fetch the other telly from our bedroom.

Mr Charlton Two television sets?

Pop Three actually.

Montgomery and Primrose go out to fetch the second television set

Mr Charlton Now, Mr Larkin, leaving aside the children for the moment, what would you estimate ——

A volley of fifty revolver shots from the television set drowns the rest of Mr Charlton's sentence

Pop What would I what?

Mr Charlton Of course, this is confidential ——

More shots

— but what would you estimate your income to be?

Pop Estimate? Income? Income? Hear that, Ma? Income!

Ma roars with laughter

Ma Outcome more likely.

Pop Six kids to feed and clothe. This place to run. Fodder to buy. Wheat as dear as gold. Horses eating their heads off. Pig-food enough to frighten you to death. Vets' fees. Fowl pest. Swine fever. Foot-and-mouth. Birds dying like flies. Blimey, income, old man? Income. I should like a drop, old man. I should like a drop.

Mariette Mr Charlton, you're not eating anything. Are you sure you wouldn't like some pineapple? Or something else? A boiled egg?

Mr Charlton (*carried away again*) Actually I'd adore a boiled egg.
Pop We got Mr Charlton eating at last. Have a brace, Mr Charlton. Have two.
Mr Charlton Thanks awfully.
Mariette Soft or hard?

Mr Charlton is again reduced to mesmeric gropings by this simple question

Mr Charlton Oh! Soft, please.
Mariette I'll do them right away.

Mariette goes to get water to boil the eggs and returns during the following

Ma Nice big brown 'uns! I tell you, Mr Charlton, they'll be perfick if Mariette
   does 'em — perfick.
Mr Charlton Now, Mr Larkin, about this income. This estimate ——
Pop Estimate it'll be an' all, old man. Lucky if we clear a fiver a week, Ma,
   ain't we?
Ma Fiver? I'd like to see one.
Mr Charlton Mr Larkin, I don't think you quite understand that there is a
   statutory obligation to disclose your income and that the penalties ——
Petunia
Zinnia } (*together*) We want boiled eggs too.
Ma Shush! Eat your fish and chips.
Pop Manners, manners. And elbows off the table.
Mr Charlton It's the law, Mr Larkin.
Pop All right, all right, old man. Law's law. Fair's fair. What's *your* income?
Mr Charlton Not all that much, I'm afraid. Civil servant, you know.
Pop Nice safe job, though.
Mr Charlton Well, I suppose so.
Pop Nothing like a nice safe job. As long as you're happy. Do you reckon
   you're happy?

An unhappy Mr Charlton tries yet again for the statistics he needs

Mr Charlton Supposing I put down a provisional five hundred?
Pop Hundred weeks in a year now, Ma! Hear that? Five hundred quid?
   Blimey, old man, I'm lucky if I clear five hundred ha'pennies!

*At this moment Montgomery and Primrose bear into the room a television
set even larger and more expensive than the first*

*While they plug in this set to replace the other, Mr Charlton tries yet again
to proceed with the filling in of the buff-yellow tax-form*

Mr Charlton Now can we have the names of the children?
Pop Well, starting with the youngest, there's Victoria.
Ma Came in plum-time. Then there's the twins — Zinnia and Petunia.
Pop Ma's favourite flowers. Then there's Primrose.
Ma I had her in the spring. Right pickle that one was.
Pop Had her head in a book ever since. Then there's Montgomery — named after the General, of course. And our eldest daughter, Mariette. Here, I always forget, Ma, how did we come to call her Mariette?
Ma I wanted to call her after that queen. I always felt sorry for that queen.
Mr Charlton Which queen?
Ma The French one. Marie Antionette. But Pop said it was too long. He'd never say it, he said.
Pop 'Course. We put the two together.

Ma looks earnestly at Mr Charlton

Ma I've been looking at you, Mr Charlton. Are you quite sure you're all right? You look as if you don't get enough to eat by half.
Mr Charlton I live in lodgings.
Pop What you want is a week or two out here. Beautiful out here. Up in our wood the nightingales sing all night long.
Mr Charlton "The wakeful nightingale". Of course — "she all night long her amorous descant sings."
Pop All night *and* all day. Like everything else in the mating season they go hell for leather.
Mr Charlton I am quite prepared to believe everything does go hell for leather, Mr Larkin, but at the moment that is not the important thing. The important thing is this form. You must fill in this form.
Pop Grub, that's what you want, old man. More grub. Plenty o' grub. Wouldn't be half so touchy if you got more grub inside you. Would he, Ma?
Ma Course not. Mariette — drop another egg in, dear!
Mr Charlton I do not want another egg.
Zinnia } (*together*) { Sometimes we have moorhens' eggs for tea.
Petunia }   { Do you like moorhens' eggs?
Mr Charlton I have never eaten a moorhen's egg in my life. Mr Larkin ——
Zinnia We know where there's a nest.
Petunia It's got six in. If you leave one she'll go on laying all summer.
Mr Charlton Mr Larkin, I must impress on you once again that there is a statutory obligation on your part to fill in this form. It is the law. Failure to do so may incur a heavy fine or imprisonment or indeed both.
Pop Hear that, Ma? Going to shove me in the Scrubs now for doing nothing.
Mr Charlton Precisely. The law says you must fill in the form and you have not filled in the form.

Pop Well, that's a bit of a lark, ain't it? I don't get no form, so I can't fill it in. You don't fill it in and now you're going to shove me inside.

Mr Charlton I did not say we were to going to shove you — I mean I have merely pointed out to you the penalties you *may* incur ——

Petunia Goose eggs are nice too.

Zinnia Do you like goose eggs?

Mr Charlton I do not like ... Mr Larkin, may I explain the whole matter to you very simply? The fact that you fill in the form does not necessarily mean that you will *have* to pay any tax ——

Pop I should think not, old man, I should think not. What do you say, Ma?

Ma I should like. Have a job to make ends meet now.

Mr Charlton In fact the allowances for the children alone will probably preclude any such possibility ——

Pop Probably what?

Mr Charlton Preclude.

Pop And what the pipe does that mean?

Mr Charlton Preclude? It means — er — to rule out. It means it won't happen.

Pop One minute I'm in the Scrubs. Next minute it won't happen.

Mr Charlton Mr Larkin, I did not make the implication ——

Pop Hear that, Ma? Implication — preclude — blimey, I never even heard words like that on the telly.

Mr Charlton Mr Larkin, it is our policy in all these matters to be fair. Firm but fair. If you will play fair with us we will play fair with you.

Pop All right: Syd Fairplay, that's me.

Mr Charlton On the other hand if you get rough and tough with us then perforce we shall have to get rough and tough with you. The Chief Inspector can be ruthless.

In delivering this impressive warning Mr Charlton endeavours, not very successfully, to look rough and tough himself

Pop Hear that, Ma? Going to use force now. Force.

Zinnia Do you like beastings?

Mr Charlton Do I like *what*?

Zinnia Beastings. It's gorgeous.

Petunia It's what you get from a cow after it's calved.

Mr Charlton is unable to speak. Far from looking rough and tough he seems about to be sick. The sight of Mariette, glamorous and gay, bearing three boiled eggs, and a plate of bread and butter doesn't help him at all

Ma Here comes Mariette with the eggs. Monty, turn up the contrast a bit. And fetch me my Guinness.

Mariette puts down the boiled eggs in front of Mr Charlton

Mariette I cut a few slices of thin bread and butter for you. I thought you'd
like that.

Zinnia } (*together*) We want some of your egg!
Petunia

Mr Charlton Thank you. Thank you very much.

*The twins now assail Mr Charlton with hungry joy, one sitting on one of his
knees and one on the other*

They're remarkably alike, the twins, aren't they?
Pop You're quick, Mr Charlton. I must say you're quick.
Ma A few days out here would do you a power o' good.

*Mr Charlton is trying, with little success, to concentrate on his eggs. The
twins, like hungry birds, wait for their first mouthful. Monty brings Ma's
Guinness*

Pop That's right, why don't you come out here and spend a day or two with
us. Ma, what are we having for dinner on Sunday? Turkey?
Ma What you like. Just what you fancy.

Zinnia } (*together*) { Roast pork! We want roast pork.
Petunia   { With brown onions!

*Mr Charlton, surprised by the intensity of this demand, fails to save his first
spoonful of egg, which is devoured by Zinnia while Petunia waits hungrily
for hers*

Mariette Or goose. What about a goose? Nobody cooks goose like Ma.
Ma I tell you what. We'll have goose *and* pork. Then I can make apple sauce
for both.
Pop Perfick. Perfick. Primrose, pass me the tomato ketchup. I got a bit of iced
bun to finish up.

*Primrose passes the tomato ketchup, which Pop pours on his bun. Mr
Charlton makes yet another unsuccessful attempt to eat a spoonful of egg*

Ma Dinner on Sunday, then, Mr Charlton. About two o'clock.
Pop What shall we have, Ma? Two geese? Or three? (*He gives an almighty
belch*) Manners. Wind's changed.
Ma Better say three.
Mr Charlton Do you really mean it, Mrs Larkin? Asking me to dinner? I
mean lunch.

Mr Charlton pauses in the act of dipping a piece of bread and butter into his egg and naturally loses it to the twins

Pop Course she means it, old man. I'm off to catch the geese and wring their ruddy necks any moment now. Nobody's birthday, Sunday, is it?
Mariette Nobody's birthday till August. I'll be eighteen then.

Mariette and Mr Charlton exchange a shy smile at this

Pop Pity it's nobody's birthday. We might have had a few fireworks.
Zinnia
Petunia } (*together*) We want to have fireworks!
Pop Mr Charlton, why don't you finish your eggs up and let Mariette take you as far as the bluebell wood and hear them nightingales?
Ma That's a good idea. I'll have tea ready by the time you get back.
Mr Charlton Tea? I thought this was tea.
Pop Blimey, old man, give us a chance, this is only dinner.
Ma You'll take Mr Charlton as far as the bluebell wood, won't you, dear?
Mariette It's a lovely idea. I'll just go and change into a dress. It's getting a little warm for jodhpurs. That's unless you'd rather ride? There's a spare pony I can have and you can take my mare.
Mr Charlton No, thanks, no. I'd prefer to walk.
Mariette All right.

At the door she pauses for an aside with Ma

Mariette Ma, could I have a spot of your Chanel Number Five?
Ma 'Course, dear. Or else the Goya. The gardenia. Try that. They both stand near my jewel-box in the bedroom.
Mariette Thanks, Ma. (*Louder*) I'll be back in a jiff.

Mariette goes

Pop Well, I must get on.
Mr Charlton Mr Larkin, I really don't think ——
Pop Got to go now, old man. Got to get the geese killed.

Pop blandly departs

Mr Charlton I have to make some sort of report ——
Zinnia
Petunia } (*together*) No more egg left!

Deftly they turn over the three eggshells so that they look like new

Ma Going for your holiday soon, Mr Charlton? Where do you usually go?

Bewildered completely, Mr Charlton goes to dip his spoon into an egg, only to find new frustration. The twins shriek with laughter

Mr Charlton I really hadn't thought ——
Ma Why don't you come strawberry picking with us? Earn a packet of money and have a nice holiday too. We start picking next Monday.
Mr Charlton But I've an office to go to. I've a job. My chief would never hear of it. He's a stickler for routine.
Ma Sounds like a bit of a horse-facer, this chief of yours. Don't sound human. Still, don't suppose tax men ever are.
Mr Charlton I know that that is the popular conception of us, Mrs Larkin. But I assure you it's quite untrue. We are human. Just as human as you and Mr Larkin.

Ma roars with laughter

Ma I must tell Pop that one. He'll like that. (*She stops laughing.*) Human, is he, your chief? Then what's he doing making you drag to work day after day in that stuffy office where you've got one foot in the grave?
Mr Charlton (*faintly*) Got what ... ?
Ma You look like a television screen without the picture on. You've got that green look.
Mr Charlton I have?
Ma Pop had a sister who looked like that. Like a green strawberry. Worked in an office just like you. Ended up not having enough strength to kiss her husband good-night. Let alone anything else.
Mr Charlton Mrs Larkin, I feel perfectly well. I feel perfectly happy.
Ma Then you don't look it. What do they give you to eat in them lodgings?
Mr Charlton The food is plain but nutritious.
Ma I'll bet it is an' all. You wait till Sunday and see what three plates o' roast goose'll do for you. I bet you weigh lighter than a sack of feathers. Puff of wind, you'd blow away.
Mr Charlton I assure you my feet are quite firmly on the ground, Mrs Larkin.
Ma (*lyrically*) When the strawberry picking's over there'll be cherries. Best cherries in the world here. Big, fat, black, juicy sweet ones. Then plums. Then damsons. Then pears. Then apples. Lovely. It's like the Garden of Eden here, Mr Charlton, only more so. Adam and Eve never enjoyed themselves half as much as we do ——

Mariette comes in. She looks more attractive than ever in a shapely dress of lime-green shantung

Mariette Ready Mr Charlton?

A stunned Mr Charlton manages to get to his feet

Lovely to have a dress on again. Lovely to feel the wind blowing round your legs.

Mr Charlton stares with palpitating bewilderment

Ma You look smashing, dear. Off you go. (*To the other children*) And you too, Montgomery, go and get your goats milked. Zinnia and Petunia, off you go and feed the hens. Primrose and Victoria, start washing up.

The children all disappear with great obedience

Ma follows to the door

Everybody's got to work here, Mr Charlton, so's we can scratch a living.

Ma goes too

A thoroughly confused Mr Charlton awaits some sort of word from the astral vision of Mariette

Mariette You didn't believe that nightingales sang all day, did you?
Mr Charlton Well, actually, no ——
Mariette Shall I tell you something else you didn't believe?
Mr Charlton What was that?
Mariette You didn't believe I could be the same girl you saw riding at Easter, did you?
Mr Charlton As a matter of fact, I didn't. How did you know?
Mariette I could see it in your eyes. I was watching you. You thought I was someone else, didn't you?
Mr Charlton Well, in point of fact, I was told — I was assured — or rather I was led to believe — that you were a niece of Lady Planson-Forbes — you know — at Carrington Hall ——

Mariette laughs seductively

Mariette And now you've found I'm not.
Mr Charlton Yes.
Mariette Does it make any difference?
Mr Charlton Well, in point of fact ——
Mariette I'm just the same girl, aren't I? I'm just me. (*She laughs again*) Come on, let's go and see if you know a nightingale when you hear one.

Mr Charlton You know, I really have to get your father to sign this tax form before I leave ——
Mariette (*laughing again*) You'll have to sign it for him. Or Ma will. Pop can't write his name.

Mariette and Mr Charlton go out to the wood. Ma comes back to the table and starts packing up the dirty dishes and the various bits of debris. Occasionally she glances at the television set, which is still on in spite of the fact that most of its audience have disappeared. Pop then appears, carrying three fat dead geese

Pop I see Mariette and Mr Charlton have gone to the bluebell wood. Beautiful up there. Nightingales singing. Cuckoos calling all the time. Good to be alive.

Among the debris from the table Ma picks up a tax form and looks at it

Ma, I think I'll get a few bottles o' port in for Sunday. So we can celebrate.
Ma Celebrate? Celebrate what?
Pop Mariette and the baby.
Ma Shhh! That's a secret.

Ma laughs like a jelly. Pop stares towards the bluebell wood, lost in contemplation of the May evening's exquisite light

Pop Only thing I hope is she won't ever want to leave here. I don't know what I'd do if she went away from here. One minute you're dangling them on your knee and then suddenly they're grown-up and you don't seem to have noticed. She's such a beautiful girl — everything a dad could wish for.

While Pop is lost in his thoughts Ma finishes clearing up the debris. Her last act is to drop Mr Charlton's empty eggshells into a waste-paper basket — together with the tax form, torn into little pieces. The way she does this leaves absolutely no doubt that she has often done the same thing before

You know what, Ma? It's paradise here. Our place. It's perfick.

Ma moves to put her arms around him from behind and they stand together looking out across the yard at their own piece of paradise

Perfick. You couldn't wish for nothing more perfick nowhere.

CURTAIN

SCENE 2

The same. Later in the evening of the same day

When the CURTAIN *rises, Pop, Ma and Mariette, in the living-room, are trying to teach Mr Charlton the mysteries of cribbage. The television set is still on, but without sound. Ma is drinking Guinness. Mariette and Mr Charlton have a glass of cider each. Pop is opening a bottle of beer from the fridge*

During the scene the light fades to reveal a sky full of brilliant stars

Pop Very fine game, crib, Mr Charlton. Very old. I'm sorry you don't get the hang of it yet. Been playing it in our family for years. How about a drop of Dragon's Blood, Mr Charlton? Very good beer.

Mr Charlton You know, I honestly think I ought to be getting home.

Mariette Tomorrow's Saturday. You don't have to go to the office Saturday, do you?

Pop Course he don't. Offices don't work Saturdays. They don't none of 'em know what work is no more.

He brings his glass of Dragon's Blood to the table, where Ma is shuffling the cards

Cut for crib, Ma. We'll show Mr Charlton another hand or two. Then I'll mix us all a cocktail.

Ma You don't want no more. You'll want to get out in the night.

Pop I'm thirsty. I'm parched up.

Ma cuts the cards; Pop also cuts — remarkably swiftly

Ace high. My crib.

But Ma is quicker. She is too well acquainted with Pop to be caught by that one. With her customary imperturbability she takes the cards and gets ready to deal

Ma Sharp as a packet o' pins. Three for no box.

Pop Always got to be using your loaf at this game, Mr Charlton. Always remember that.

Ma deals out five cards each

By the way, what is your other name? Can't go on calling you Mister
Charlton all the time. (*He takes a quick look at his cards*) Mis-deal. Six
cards. Bung in.

Ma Pick 'em up! Don't you dare.

Pop Terrible hand. Needed a Parson's Poke.

Ma No more Parson's Pokes. Cut! Get on with it. Two for his heels. Make
the best with what you've got.

Ma playfully kicks Mr Charlton under the table

Always got to watch him, Mr Charlton. Want eyes in the back of your head.
What did you say your name was?

Mr Charlton Cedric.

*Ma chokes on her Guinness. Pop leaps up and gives her a severe blow in the
middle of the back, at the same time taking a good look at her cards*

Pop Steady, girl. Steady. Often happens to Ma. She's got a very small gullet
compared to the rest of her. All right now, Ma?

Ma recovers and nods that she is all right

Seen her choke over a hair on a gooseberry. (*Laying a card*) Eight. I tell you
what — how about calling you Charley?

Mr Charlton Please call me Charley if you wish.

Mariette (*laying a card*) Fifteen.

Mr Charlton Nine?

Ma No, twenty-four. Seven's a score.

Pop Ma's away. Three.

Mariette Two of 'em.

Mr Charlton Eleven?

Ma You're learning. Nineteen. And a go.

Mariette Fifteen two, fifteen four, and a pair's six. Your take now, Charley.

Mr Charlton One, two, three, four. Will that do?

Ma Fifteen two, fifteen four, and four's eight. That's the spirit, Charley.

Pop Beginner's luck. More than I've got. (*He throws down his hand.*) Damn
all. What Paddy shot at. Yes, Charley suits you.

Ma Fifteen two, fifteen four, pair's six, three's nine and three's twelve.(*She
pegs her score on the peg-board and then looks at the cards in her box*)
Two, three's five and three's eight. And one for his nob. Nine.

Pop Getting the hang of it now, Charley boy?

Mr Charlton I don't quite understand this "one for his nob".

Pop Jack. Knave. I told you. One for his nob. Two for his heels.

Mariette Oh! I'm tired of crib. We've been playing for hours and Mr Charlton still doesn't understand it.

Pop now goes over to the cocktail cabinet, from which he takes up a book. When Pop opens the cabinet, it plays a tune

Pop I thought you was an office man, Charley? I thought you was good at figures.

Mr Charlton Rather different sort of figures, I'm afraid. Am I wrong — or is it in the shape of a ship?

Pop Spanish galleon. Heigh-ho and a bottle of rum. Very good book I got here too. Montgomery gave it me for Christmas. About the only book I ever get time to read. "A Guide to Better Drinking".

Ma Funny how you miss telly when you're talking. You feel lost somehow. Do you feel lost, Mr Charlton?

Mr Charlton not only looks lost, but greatly bewildered. He seems to be breathing heavily

Mariette Something the matter, Mr Charlton?

Mr Charlton It's this extraordinary perfume. What is it?

Mariette Gardenia. It's Ma's.

She leans her face nearer to Mr Charlton, who takes a deep, confused and intoxicating breath

Do you like it?

Mr Charlton (*shaken, ecstatic and completely lost*) Like it? Like it? I — I ... (*He suddenly gets up, determined to take a firm grip on himself*). It's absolutely no use. I must go.

Ma Go?

Mariette Go? Why?

Mr Charlton It's no use. I must. I'm absolutely adamant.

Pop (*stunned by this word*). Absolutely what?

Mr Charlton Adamant. Absolutely adamant.

Pop Blimey, that's another word I never heard on telly.

Mr Charlton I must catch my bus ——

Pop Last bus has gone, old man.

Ma They took it off when petrol rationing came in and they never put it back again.

Pop Stay the night.

Mr Charlton I've nothing with me. Nothing to wear. No pyjamas.

Pop Gawd A'mighty. Pyjamas?

Pop stares in awe and admiration at Mr Charlton, who wears pyjamas to sleep in and uses words never even heard on television

Sleep in your shirt, old man. Like I do.

Ma You can have one of my nighties!

Mariette I wear pyjamas. I'll lend you a pair of mine.

Mr Charlton No, really, really ——

Ma Go upstairs and fetch a pair, dear, and we'll see if they fit, and while you're at it — pop the mattress on the billiard table. We can fix the covers later.

Mariette goes

Mr Charlton Billiard table?

Pop Don't be long. Drinks won't be half a jiff. (*He has been searching the "Guide to Better Drinking" for a recipe. He now produces one*) How about this one, Ma? Here's one we never tried. "Rolls-Royce".

While Pop mixes the cocktail Mr Charlton searches for his briefcase

Ma Very stylish, I'm sure.

Pop Half vermouth, quarter whisky, quarter gin, dash of orange bitters.

Ma Dash you will too, with that lot. It'll blow your head off.

Pop Blow summat off. Not sure what, though.

Ma laughs like a jelly

(*Mixing the cocktail*) Well, here goes. Try anything once, that's what I say.

Ma Talking about Rolls-Royce, Pop, did you do anything about that one you were after?

Pop Sunday. Chap who owns it's a stockbroker. Only comes down from London weekends. I'll see him then.

Ma Pop's mad on having a Rolls, Mr Charlton.

She suddenly stops. Mr Charlton has seized the opportunity to get his fountain pen and fill in yet another tax form

Ma What are you up to?

Mr Charlton I *must* get this form filled in. I simply must. It's absolutely imperative. And then I must go home.

Pop looks sharply up, again astonished at the range of Mr Charlton's vocabulary. He makes no comment, however, but turns to the cocktail

Pop Well, cocktails are ready. (*He pours them out into four smart tumblers*)
Mixed 'em double. Saves time.
Ma Better try it yourself first. We don't want it if it's no good, Rolls-Royce
or no Rolls-Royce. Besides you might fall down dead.

Pop takes a good swig at the cocktail

Pop Perfick. Absolutely perfick. This'll grow hair all right. Well, roll on
Monday. Here's to the strawberry lark.
Ma You really ought to come strawberry picking, Mr Charlton. Earn
yourself fifteen or twenty quid and all the strawberries you can eat. You can
gather a hundred and fifteen pounds in no time.

Pop shakes his head at Ma going on about what she can earn

Pop In a good season, Ma. In a good season.
Ma Oh, yeah. A really good season. Usually it's only pennies, of course.
Mr Charlton Seems to me an awful lot of money gets paid out to these
people. These pickers. Strawberries, cherries, hops and so on. Strictly in
law they ought to pay tax.
Pop Pay tax?
Mr Charlton I mean, if the law is to be interpreted in the strict letter ——
Pop Strick letter, my aunt Fanny. Dammit, Charley, if they was taxed they
wouldn't come. Simple as that. Then you wouldn't have no strawberries,
no cherries, no apples, no nothink. No beer even!
Mr Charlton Oh.

Pop sets down Mr Charlton's drink rather sharply

Pop You have to use your loaf, Charley. Use your loaf and life will be good
to you. That's my motto. Cheers.
Mr Charlton Cheers.

*Absentmindedly Mr Charlton reaches out with his free hand, grabs the
tumbler and drinks. Instantly a draught of pure alcohol paralyses him
completely, making him speechless. He tries to rise to his feet. His eyes
wobble, wet with tears. He grasps at the edges of the table, shaking. A few
forlorn broken sounds stutter from his lips and die*

Pop Perfick pick me up, this. We must all have some more o' this. Eh, Mr
Charlton?
Mr Charlton I — I — I ...

Mariette comes in, carrying a pair of very bright flowered pyjamas

Through tearful eyes Mr Charlton watches her come towards him

Mariette I'll just try them against you for size. (*She holds the pyjama jacket against him*) Stand up straight.
Mr Charlton I — I — I — I ... (*He makes a shaky attempt to stand upright*)
Mariette Lovely. They might have been made for you.
Pop Perfick. Suit you down to the ground, Charley boy.

Mr Charlton, in fact, almost falls to the ground

Well, cheers, everybody. Cheers.
Ma Cheers. A few more of these and you won't see me for dust.
Mr Charlton A — few — more? A ...
Pop Refill coming up in a minute. (*He goes over to the cocktail cabinet*) Bet this would go well with a bloater paste sandwich, Ma? Anybody feel peckish?

While he starts to mix the second round of cocktails Mariette moves closer to Mr Charlton, speaking softly and bewitchingly

Mariette Have you made up your mind to come strawberry picking with us on Monday?

A wave of Gardenia floats across Mr Charlton's face. He breathes it deeply, half closing his eyes. She sits down at his side

I'm sure you'd love it. Especially if you've never done it before.

Mr Charlton takes refuge in drink. His deep swig at the cocktail half-paralyses him a second time

If you couldn't come all day you could come in the evenings. Lots of people do. It's lovely in the evenings. Listening to the nightingales and hearing the cuckoo. Do you like the cuckoo?
Mr Charlton (*drunkenly*) "Summer is acumen in. Loudly sing cuckoo!"

Pop takes a taste of the newly mixed cocktail

Pop Ah! Perfick. (*He smacks his lips appreciatively*) More perfick than ever!
Ma Wants just a wee bit of ice in it next time, I should say.
Pop Right. I'll get it.

Mr Charlton, seeing an opportunity for temporary escape, swiftly drains his glass and gets up

Mr Charlton No, I'll get it. I'm the ice-man. That's me.

Already inspired by alcohol, a slightly uninhibited Mr Charlton half leaps away to fetch the ice

Pop I don't think he's a bad feller, Mr Charlton, when you get to know him.
Ma Wants plenty of feeding up and fresh air, that's all. How'd you get on, duckie? In the bluebell woods?
Mariette Slow. He's very shy.
Ma Well, he mustn't be shy. That won't get him nowhere. Last place you wanna be shy is in the bluebell woods.
Mariette He would talk about horses.

Ma pulls a face, clearly unimpressed

Mr Charlton bears a tray of ice-cubes

Mr Charlton Ice coming up! Ice coming up!

Pop strikes him with sudden friendliness on the back

Pop Just saying what a rattlin' good feller you are, Charley boy. Next time you come out you must bring your car. What kind of car you got?
Mr Charlton I don't have a car.
Pop No car? That'll never do. See if I can lay my hands on a little run-about for you. Everybody should have a car.
Mr Charlton I'm afraid I can't drive.
Mariette I'll teach you.
Mr Charlton Oh, thank you, Mariette. That would — that would be terrific.
Mariette Terrific.
Mr Charlton (*besotted*) Terrific.
Pop Everybody got drinks, that's the main thing? Charley boy, bring your glasses and let me fill 'em up.

Mr Charlton goes over to have his and Mariette's glasses filled up

Pop All right, Charley boy?
Mr Charlton Excellent! Splendid!
Pop That's the spirit.

He strikes Mr Charlton another severe, friendly blow on the back. A groping Mr Charlton, less and less inhibited every moment, goes back to Mariette. He actually blunders against her and half sits on her lap. She pulls him down and keeps him there

Mr Charlton (*raising his glass to eye-level with exuberant enthusiasm*) "And beaded bubbles winking at the brim!" Cheers! Happy days! (*He drinks recklessly*)

Ma, inspired by Mr Charlton sitting on Mariette's lap, goes over and sits on Pop's. The two couples are quiet for some moments. Pop has in fact, completely disappeared under the enormous bulk of Ma. In the ensuing silence Mariette starts to rock Mr Charlton gently backwards and forwards. Mr Charlton is in a dream. He comes out of it at last to find that there is no sign of Pop

Where's Pop gone? I didn't see Pop go out.

Ma shrieks with laughter

Pop Under here!
Ma Under me. I'm sitting on his lap.
Pop Next best place to being in bed.
Ma Bed? We're not going to bed yet. We only just got going.
Pop Early start tomorrow. Load of hay to deliver. Then I got to pick up the new deep-freeze. And the pigs. And the port. Charley boy, I've been thinking. This might be your last chance to come in on the strawberry lark.
Mr Charlton Why is that?
Pop Strawberries are dying out. Won't be no strawberries soon. Disease.
Mr Charlton Actually I prefer raspberries myself.
Pop The raspberry lark's nearly over too. Mosaic. Weakening strain. And the plum lark. And the apple lark. They can't sell apples for love nor money——
Mr Charlton What about gardenias? What about the gardenia lark? (*He laughs half-hysterically*). When do we pick the gardenias?
Pop So it might be your last chance, Charley-boy. What about it? Are you coming?
Mr Charlton (*with rising abandon*) Coming? Of course I'm coming! I'll come in the evenings, when the cuckoo calls ——
Mariette Oh! Lovely!
Mr Charlton "Oh, cuckoo, shall I call thee bird?"
Pop Good-oh! That calls for another round. Ma, let me get up.

Ma heaves her great weight off Pop, who at once goes to the cocktail cabinet and takes up the "Guide to Better Drinking"

Mariette It's sweet of you to say you'll come. Do you really mean it?
Mr Charlton There ought to be a cocktail called "Gardenia".

Pop I'll invent one.
Mr Charlton And one called "Mariette". A sweet one.
Pop What about this one? Chauffeur? Dammit, the Rolls has to have a chauffeur. One third vermouth, one third whisky, one third gin, dash of angostura. Sounds perfick. Everybody game?
Mr Charlton Everybody game!
Pop Perfick. I'll mix 'em double again.

While Mr Charlton rocks on Mariette's knee, Pop mixes up another large cocktail. When this is ready, he calls Mr Charlton

Come and taste it, Charley boy.

With unsteady alacrity Mr Charlton gets up from Mariette's knee and goes over to Pop, who pours out a tumbler of the new cocktail

There y'are. Try that for size.

Mr Charlton drinks with deep appraisal

Mr Charlton Nectar!

Pop instantly fills up Mr Charlton's glass and then his own. Then he goes over to first Ma, then Mariette, and gives them their drinks. When this is finished he is moved to stand by the door and gaze out into the May night for a few moments in silent ecstasy

Pop Perfick night. Perfick. You can hear the stars breathing.
Mr Charlton (*drinking*) Enchanting.
Pop Nightingales still going hell for leather.
Mr Charlton (*drinking again*) Ravishing.
Pop Perfick. Absolutely perfick ——

There is a sudden loud bang. It is the sound of Mr Charlton falling flat on his face. This catastrophe upsets neither Ma nor Pop very much. Nor is Mariette greatly perturbed as she gets up and picks up the pyjamas

Ma I said all along he wasn't very strong.
Pop Ups-a-daisy, Charley boy.

He and Mariette pick up the nearly unconscious Mr Charlton

Mariette Mattress is all ready on the billiard table.

Mariette starts to bear Mr Charlton away. Mr Charlton stops and looks at her

Mr Charlton "Shall I compare thee to a summer's day? Thou art more lovely and more temperate. Rough winds do shake the darling buds of May ..."
Pop Poetry again, I shouldn't wonder.
Ma Want any help, dear? Or can you manage by yourself?
Mariette I think I can manage.
Ma Well, call if you want me.
Mariette Come on, off we go.
Mr Charlton You're my goose. You're my gardenia.

Mariette goes out with Charley and the pyjamas

Ma takes a calm sip or two of her drink and then drifts like a huge, soft, undisturbed balloon towards the door. Gazing at the night outside, she at last steps out into the yard

Pop Think I'll have a cigar.

He searches under the cocktail cabinet for something, finds it and then picks up his drink. He joins Ma outside, carrying his glass in one hand, his cigar in the other

That's another thing I have in common with Mr Churchill. I like a good cigar.

Together he and Ma stand silent before the dark altar of the night. He sets down his drink on an empty oil drum and starts to light up his cigar

Going to wear your pink nightgown tonight, Ma?
Ma I generally do, Friday nights, don't I?
Pop Jolly good. Perfick.

A few more seconds of silence pass. Pop blows smoke but is frowning slightly

Nothing wrong, is there, Ma? Not worried about anything?
Ma Oh, I was just thinking.
Pop Oh! What about?
Ma Mr Charlton.
Pop Oh! He'll be all right. Sleep as sound as a dormouse. Do him good.
Ma It wasn't that.
Pop Oh? What was it?
Ma I was just wondering if that young man knows his technique.

Ma and Pop stand wondering about the implications of this important aspect of Mr Charlton's character as the Lights slowly fade

CURTAIN

SCENE 3

The same. Sunday morning, two days later

Church bells ring in the distance. A brilliant morning. The yard scintillates under the heat of noon. A table has been set out under the chestnut tree. At one end of it sits Mariette, reading the News of the World. *At the other end sits Mr Charlton, reading the* Sunday Express. *Mr Charlton is in his shirtsleeves and wearing dark glasses, but otherwise seems very much as before. Mariette looks, if anything, even more attractive than she did. She is wearing near sky-blue linen shorts and an open-necked vermilion blouse. Ma is in the house, cooking the geese for Sunday dinner. She is wearing a vast canary-yellow pinafore with big scarlet pockets*

From their absorption in the newspapers if seems clear that Mariette and Mr Charlton have not succeeded in becoming much more intimately acquainted with each other

Ma comes to the door and stares at them in puzzled disappointment, if not disgust, slowly shaking her head

Ma What vegetables do you two fancy? I already got asparagus, green peas, new potatoes, roast potatoes, braised onions and broad beans. If there's anything else you'd like you'd better say now. I'd hate anybody to go hungry.

Mariette and Mr Charlton make no sign that they have heard

What's it like under the tree? Hot?

Again no sign or answer from Mariette and Mr Charlton. Now Ma shouts at them

Cedric! I said is it hot under the tree?

An apologetic and startled Mr Charlton drops his newspaper and hastily gets up

Mr Charlton Oh, no, Mrs Larkin, cool. Beautifully cool. Deliciously cool.
Ma Looks like it too. All right, we'll have dinner out there. Too blinking hot
in the kitchen. You and Mariette put the papers away and get the table laid.
It's gone twelve o'clock. Pop'll be back any moment now, hungry as two
starving cart horses.
Mr Charlton Yes, Mrs Larkin. Certainly. Certainly.

Mariette is still absorbed in her paper

Ma Mariette!
Mariette Yes, Ma. Just coming.

Mr Charlton goes into the house

Ma and Mariette are left alone for a moment

Ma (*with sarcasm*) Must be interesting papers this morning.
Mariette He's so shy.
Ma Well, you mustn't let him be shy, must you? You must stimulate him.
Somehow. At least he's still here.
Mariette I don't think he knows what happened to Saturday.
Ma Lost day?
Mariette Gone for ever. Said it was his very first and last hangover.
Ma Not in this family, it won't be.
Mariette Have you noticed? His eye-lashes are just like little brown paint-
brushes.

*With this remark, said half in a dream, Mariette goes past her mother into the
house. Ma shrugs her shoulders, mystified, and follows her*

*Mr Charlton comes into the yard, carrying a tablecloth and a tray of cutlery
and glasses. He takes these to the table. Just as he is about to set it down, the
low, distinguished, honeyed sound of a motor horn comes from off stage. Mr
Charlton abruptly stops and listens. When the motor horn stops he proceeds
to set down the tray a second time. This time he is arrested by a very different
sound — a positive, peremptory snarl from the same direction as the first. It
too comes from a motor horn. Mr Charlton is so startled that he drops the tray*

The various sounds bring Ma and Mariette running excitedly from the house

Ma Must be Pop.
Mariette He's got the Rolls!

Ma takes off her apron, throws it over Charley's shoulder and smoothes back her hair

Ma Hold the fort, Charley.

They run across the yard and disappear

Excited voices, including those of the children, can be heard from the same direction as the notes of the motor horn. Mr Charlton, uncertain as to what to do, starts to follow Mariette and Ma, then decides against it and starts to busy himself with the glass and cutlery. Every few seconds the sound of the motor startles him again — first the long, distinguished, honeyed note, then the peremptory, urgent snarl. Finally Mr Charlton can resist it no longer. Apron round his neck, he starts to walk across the yard. He is half-way across it when:

The Brigadier appears from the opposite direction. The Brigadier is more than six feet tall: sixtyish, thin, straight as a straw, with eyebrows and moustaches that bristle like salty prawns. He wears a yellowish tropical suit that seems to have been run over by a steam-roller. The suit is also much patched and has shrunk badly, revealing socks that are not a pair. One is white, the other yellow. On the back of his head he wears a hat that looks very much like a frayed bee-skip. He speaks in cryptic tones, not without humour

Brigadier Morning.
Mr Charlton Oh! Good-morning.
Brigadier Larkin at home?
Mr Charlton I rather fancy he's just arrived.

The motor horn gives another startling exhibition in both tones

Brigadier Good God, what was that?
Mr Charlton That, I think is Mr Larkin. I'll tell him you're here. What name shall I say?
Brigadier Just tell him it's the General. He'll know.

Mr Charlton retires in the direction of the motor horn, his confused progress speeded by yet another exhibition of honey-and-snarl and a following chorus of excited Larkin voices

The Brigadier, while waiting, stares in mute unbelief at the interior of the Larkin household

Pop comes in, breezily. He is dressed in an orange shirt, dark green slacks and a flat beige cap. In contrast to the seedy, decaying Brigadier, he looks remarkably smart

Pop Ah! General, General, General. Morning, morning, morning. Perfick wevver.
Brigadier Hail. Well met, Larkin.

They shake hands

Pop Didn't know you were here. Only just arrived myself. Something I can do for you?
Brigadier Well I just walked over ——
Pop Walked? What's wrong with the car?
Brigadier Nothing. Sold it, that's all.
Pop Flogged it? No!
Brigadier Had to. No alternative. Can't afford the petrol. Can't afford a man to clean it. Can't get a man even if I could afford it. No option — time I did more walking anyway.
Pop No car? That's bad. That's very bad.

The urgent snarl shatters the morning air yet again

Brigadier Good God, Larkin, what *is* that?
Pop My Rolls. Just got it. Marvellous. Got one horn for town work — one you just heard — another for the country. And monograms on the door, General! Monograms on the doors!
Brigadier Good God. Royal?
Pop No. Duke, I think. Duke, Viscount, Earl or summat o' that breed. And a speaking tube, General, a speaking tube.
Brigadier Hellish costly to run?
Pop Pay for itself in no time. Pay for itself in prestige.
Brigadier Suppose so.
Pop Only thing, Ma says they'll put the price of fish and chips up when they see us coming. Snifter?
Brigadier Trifle early don't you think? Not quite over the yard-arm yet, are we?
Pop When I want a drink, General, I have a drink. Wevver it's early or wevver it ain't.
Brigadier I honestly mustn't linger. As a matter of fact, I came to ——
Pop Bet a quid you want a subscription.
Brigadier Wrong. Not this time.
Pop Well, that's worth a drink. What'll it be? Whisky?

Brigadier If you insist.
Pop Good. I'll have a Dragon's Blood. With a dash of lime.

Pop goes into the house to get the drinks. As he mixes and pours them at the cocktail cabinet he carries on talking to the Brigadier through the open door

You're looking a bit pale round the gills, General. Nothing wrong, I hope?
Quite fit, old man?
Brigadier So-so. But over-worked, I expect.
Pop Over-worked? I never thought you did any. Thought you were retired.
Brigadier Retired? (*He gives a hollow laugh*). Strange sort of retirement
when I can't even get a man to mow the lawn or a boy to clean the shoes.
· I used to have three batmen waiting on me at one time. Never cleaned a shoe
or brushed a suit myself for thirty years. Now I do everything from washing
up the dishes to cleaning out the drains. I'm part of the new working class.

Pop, cheerful as ever, brings out the drinks and gives the whisky to the Brigadier

Pop Well, cheers, General. Here's to more hair on your chest.
Brigadier Cheers. (*He drinks*) No, Larkin, there's nothing physically wrong
with me. Why I dropped in to see you — I'm in a God-awful mess.
Pop Wimmin?
Brigadier Good God, no. Bad enough. But not that bad.
Pop That's good. Never get into trouble with wimmin, that's my motto. Give
'em what they want, strong and often, but never get into trouble.
Brigadier No, it's this damn gymkhana.
Pop Oh! the one Mariette's practising for. She's mad about that gymkhana.
She can't sleep at nights for thinking about that. What's wrong?
Brigadier That bolshie Fortescue had a God-awful row with the committee
last Friday and has withdrawn from the field.
Pop Always was a basket.
Brigadier Not only withdrawn from the field, but withdrawn *the* field.
Pop You mean you've nowhere to hold the damn thing?
Brigadier Bingo.
Pop Selfish bloody sausage. Well, there's got to be a gymkhana, that's
certain. Mariette'll go mad if there's no gymkhana. (*He starts musing in
a lower voice, remembering the baby*) It'll very likely be the last chance
she'll get to ride before her bab ——
Brigadier Before her what? Didn't catch that, Larkin.
Pop Before her birthday, General. You can hold the damn thing in our
medder ——
Brigadier Don't let me rush you into a decision, Larkin. You don't have to
decide now ——

Pop Good grief, nothing to decide. The medder's there. All I got to do is get the grass cut. I'll get the grass cut this week and everything'll be perfick.
Brigadier Larkin, I can't thank you enough. Never be able to thank you. You're a stout feller. Stout feller. Wish there were more like you.
Pop Don't thank me, General. I'm doing it for Mariette. (*He pauses, recognizing the truth of his words*) I am an' all. Well, cheers, General. Here's to a rattlin' good day. Drink up.
Brigadier Cheers. And my eternal thanks.

They drink

Ma comes back

Ma Morning, General. Here, what's the old cook done this morning? Don't she get a snifter?
Brigadier Mrs Larkin. Madam. (*He gives a polite bow*) I trust I see you well?
Ma Hot as hell and thirsty as a bloater. How are you? How's your sister?

Pop takes the Brigadier's empty glass from his hand and goes into the house for more drinks

Brigadier Much as usual, thank you. Gone to see an aunt today. Over in Hampshire. Day's march away.
Ma Sunday dinner all on your lonesome, eh?
Brigadier Not quite that bad. I shall waffle down to the pub and grab a bite of cold.
Ma Cold on Sundays? That's awful. You wouldn't catch Pop having cold on Sundays. Why don't you stay here and eat with us?
Brigadier No, no, really. Thanks all the same, really ——

Pop comes back with drinks for Ma and the Brigadier

Pop More the merrier, General. More the merrier.
Brigadier Bless my soul, with all your brood ——
Ma Of course. Cold, my foot.
Pop That's settled then. Ma, pity you didn't put that leg o' lamb in as well as the pork and geese. Too late now, I suppose?
Ma Not unless you want to eat about five o'clock. Gorblimey, I must run. Kids'll be back from the shop in a minute. Haven't got the apple sauce made yet. (*She rushes into the house, taking her drink. Pausing and calling back to the Brigadier*). Take a peep at our Rolls, General. It's got a silver vase for flowers and a speaking tube. Home, James!

Ma goes into the kitchen

Brigadier Well, lead on, Larkin. Let's cast an eye on this fabulous machine of yours.
Pop It's got tone, General, I tell you. Beautiful tone.

Mr Charlton comes back with Mariette

Mariette Hullo, Brigadier.

She goes into the house

Brigadier (*following her all the way with his eyes*). Damned attractive girl, Larkin. Gets more attractive every time I see her.
Pop Glad somebody thinks so. Here, meet a friend of hers. Mister Charlton. Late entry. Chap from the tax-lark.
Brigadier How do you do.
Mr Charlton How do you do.
Brigadier You mean a real pukka tax-gatherer?
Pop (*with ringing laughter*) Tried to rope me in on that swindle, General. I should like, eh? What do you say?
Brigadier I'm afraid, with my beggarly pittance, I don't pay any tax.
Pop (*thundering*) And rightly so!

Mariette comes back from inside the house, goes across to the table and starts to lay the cloth. Mr Charlton joins her

Pop Oh! Charley boy, do summat for me. Ice the port, will you? Ice buckets are in the cocktail cabinet.

The Brigadier's reaction to this is one of stunned stupefaction

Brigadier Iced port?
Pop Three bottles, Charley. Two red and one white. Give 'em plenty of ice. Chill 'em well off, old man.

The Brigadier looks almost frozen too

Pop Make a very good drink mixed, General, the red and the white. Ever try it?

If there is an answer to this the Brigadier cannot find it. He starts to walk away. Pop goes too. They have not reached the other side of the yard, however, before an unexpected visitor arrives

This is the Inspector of Taxes. He is a tall, well-dressed, middle-aged man of the professional type, wearing a cream linen jacket and dark grey trousers, without a hat

Inspector Excuse me. I do hope you don't mind my intruding like this ——

Hardly has this sentence been begun before Mr Charlton, in the swiftest movement of his life, dives clean under the table and disappears

Pop Morning, morning, what can I do you for?

Inspector I wonder if I could beg a jug of water?

Pop Good God. Not to drink?

Inspector Oh! no, for my car. She suddenly started boiling up. This frightfully hot weather, I suppose. Heavens, it's hot. Hottest May for eighty years, I read. I hope it's no great trouble?

Pop No trouble at all. Charley'll get it. Charley boy, get this gentleman a can ... Where's Charley? I thought Charley was here ...

Mariette (*impassively*) He seems to have gone somewhere.

Pop Oh! well, it don't matter. Me and the General are just coming out that way. I'll get it in the yard.

Pop begins to cross the remainder of the yard with the Brigadier and the Inspector

What kind of car have you got, sir? I just happened on a very nice Rolls.

The Inspector pauses and turns back

Inspector Austin. Heavens, something smells wonderful.

Pop Bluebells. Woods are full of bluebells.

Inspector Eh? I meant the cooking.

Pop (*laughing loudly*) Oh! the geese. I got bluebells on the brain — bluebells and nightingales. Your wife with you, sir? You should take her as far as our wood before you go. Them nightingales go hell for leather all day and all night like a long-playing record and the bluebells lay everywhere like fick blue corn.

Brigadier You know, Larkin, you're something of a poet.

Pop The country gets into my blood at May-time, General, that's what it is. It gives me St Vitus' dance in the arteries.

Inspector Delicious aroma. Absolutely delicious.

Pop Tell you what. Have a look at the geese and put your name on a couple. I'll find you two nice ten-pounders that'll melt in your mouth as soft as dairy butter.

Inspector That's an idea. I'll ask my wife.
Pop Tender as a young bosom they'll be.

Pop, the Brigadier and the Inspector go

Mariette, mystified, stands alone and silent at the table. Mr Charlton makes no sign of reappearing from underneath it. Mariette waits for several seconds and then lifts the edge of the cloth

Ma comes out from the house

At this very moment Mr Charlton decides to crawl out from under the table. The two stare at each other for some seconds in silence. Ma speaks first

Ma Whatever's come over Charley?

A much shaken Mr Charlton crawls out from under the table and stands up

  Is it the sun?
Mr Charlton Not the sun, Mrs Larkin. Much worse.
Mariette A gentleman came into the yard to ask for a jug of water and all of a sudden ——
Mr Charlton I must go home.
Mariette Not again.
Ma You don't look well.
Mariette Perhaps you'd like to have a lay-down until dinner's ready.
Mr Charlton No thank you, Mariette. I must go home. (*With a shaking finger he points in the direction taken by Pop, the Inspector, and the Brigadier*) That gentleman you just saw — he's my boss — he's the Inspector of Taxes.
Ma (*unconcerned*) Oh!
Mariette He looked such a nice man too.
Mr Charlton I must catch the next bus ——

He starts to move towards the house. It is too late. Voices are heard from the direction of the Rolls Royce

Pop, the Brigadier and the Inspector come back

Mr Charlton makes the second swiftest move of his life and dives behind the chestnut tree

Inspector I'm most grateful to you. Most grateful.

Pop Well, that's it then, geese'll be ready Friday. Just in time for the weekend. Oh! by the way, my wife, my daughter Mariette — Mister — where's Charley? Charley not back yet?
Ma Morning.
Mariette How do you do.

The Inspector bows in such a way that it is not quite certain whether the gesture is towards Ma and Mariette or towards the torturing odours of roast goose

Pop Gentleman's bought two geese and'll be popping over to collect 'em on Friday. Oh! I forgot — plucked or not plucked?
Inspector Plucked, if you don't mind.
Pop Plucked it is. Ma'll do it. She's the plucking expert. Snifter before you go?
Inspector No thanks, no thanks. Must be on our way. Most grateful. Goodbye — (*He starts to go, but once again, tortured by the odours of roasting geese, he pauses and takes a deep breath*) Delicious. Must say they smell absolutely delicious.
Pop Why don't you stay and have a bite with us? No trouble.
Ma (*to Pop*) Well, I don't know ——
Inspector Oh! no, no, no. Thank you all the same.
Pop Always plenty. We're going to have it outside today. The Brigadier's staying aren't you, General?
Brigadier Thank you, a pleasure, thank you.
Mariette (*about the Inspector*) Perhaps another time?
Inspector It's very tempting, but ——
Pop The more the merrier.
Inspector I must say you tempt me ——
Pop Go on, go and get your wife. At least you can have a snifter ——
Mariette Pop ——
Inspector You're most kind. I think perhaps I will. One moment ...
Ma Pop ——

He departs. Before the tension can relax and before Mr Charlton has a chance to move the Inspector is back again

Inspector I must be raving mad. We're having lunch with my wife's mother. What on earth am I thinking about? I suppose it was some sort of defence mechanism on my part. Goodbye.

He departs in haste

A considerable pause follows

Pop What the ruddy 'ell was he talking about? Defence what?
Brigadier Defence mechanism. It's a device I'm not unfamiliar with in
dealing with my sister.
Pop Oh! Never heard of it. Not even on television.
Ma (*breathing a sigh of relief*) Well, this won't get the gravy made. Dinner'll
be five minutes now.

She goes back into the house

*Mr Charlton, still shaken, comes out from behind the tree. Pop is extremely
surprised*

Pop Hullo. What's Charley been behind the tree for? Looks as miserable as
a three-legged dog.
Mariette He doesn't feel very well.
Brigadier Touch of the sun no doubt.

Pop looks at Mr Charlton more closely

Pop Charley, what you need is a Larkin Special.
Mr Charlton I have to go home ——
Pop You need a Larkin Special, Charley, and that's what you're going to get.
Did you do the port?
Mr Charlton (*shaking his head*) No.

Pop goes into the house

*Mariette solicitously helps Mr Charlton to sit at the table. Mr Charlton is
plunged in shaken gloom. Mariette starts to finish laying the table*

Mr Charlton I must go. I must go.
Brigadier Let me help.
Mariette Oh no, General, I can manage ——
Brigadier Have to do it at home. Can't even get a washer-up. (*He starts to
lay knives and forks about the table: a rather sad, touching figure*)
Remember the time when I had two batmen, three cooks, four other maids,
a groom and a chauffeur. Never tied my own bootlaces for thirty years.
Now I clean the drains out.

*Towards the close of this speech Mr Charlton gets up and starts to creep away
across the yard. All his intentions are, however, frustrated by the noisy
arrival of the children*

Montgomery, Primrose, Victoria and the twins enter. As usual they are sucking ice-creams and eating potato crisps. They have also brought huge blocks of chocolate and raspberry mousse for lunch

Zinnia } (*together*) We want to sit next to Mr Charlton!
Petunia
Mariette Take the mousse and put it in the fridge, somebody. It'll melt here.
Montgomery I'll take it.
Mariette You can help Pop with the port too. It wants icing. And bring more chairs.

Montgomery goes into the house

Mr Charlton is forced back to the table by the superior forces of Victoria, Primrose and the twins. The girls sit at various places about the table, the twins one on each side of Mr Charlton. They offer him ice-cream. He dejectedly refuses. Victoria offers the Brigadier ice-cream. He too refuses

Primrose Have some crisps then, have some crisps.
Brigadier Thank you. (*He eats crisps*)

Pop appears, carrying a tray on which are wine glasses. He has a chair in the other hand

Pop There y'are. Another double for you, General. A Larkin Special for Charley boy. And a Red Bull for me.
Brigadier Red Bull?

Pop sets Mr Charlton's drink on the table

Pop Another one from my book, "A Guide to Better Drinking". One part whisky, one part gin, one part brandy and a dash of peach bitters.
Brigadier Good God.
Pop Blinder.

Montgomery appears carrying chairs, which he sets about the table. He goes back to the house to fetch the port

Mr Charlton meanwhile stares at his drink

Don't stare at it, Charley boy. Drink it. Knock it back. In one go. In five minutes you'll feel perfick again.

Mr Charlton still hesitates

Go on, Charley. Like this. (*He knocks back the greater part of his Red Bull in one go*)
Mariette Steady, Pop. You'll be pickled.
Pop Never been pickled in me life. Anyway not more than once or twice a week. And then only standin' up pickled.
Brigadier Is there some other form?
Pop Layin'-down pickled, o' course. Drink up, Charley boy. Down the hatch.

Mr Charlton nerves himself to drink and does. His reaction is much as it was after his first cocktail. He tries to rise but can't. He tries to speak but there are no words

Jolly good. Perfick. Well, everybody get seated. Ma says everybody get seated.

Montgomery comes back with the port, which is in two silver-plated ice-buckets. He sets them on the table

Mr Charlton is paralysed, speechless

Pop General, you sit here. You'll be next to Ma.

Pop picks up carving knife and steel and starts sharpening his knife

Mariette I don't think Charley feels at all well.
Pop Not to worry, Charley, that's the Larkin Special putting ginger into your kidneys, that's all.
Mr Charlton I — I ...
Pop You should take some leave, Charley. Take advantage of the National Elf Lark. What a swindle. I bet you've already paid millions in weekly stamps. Go sick! Have a bit of fun!
Mr Charlton Sick?
Mariette That is a good idea. You could stay a week — and then all next weekend.
Mr Charlton There'll be an awful stink if I don't get back.
Mariette There must be some way ——
Mr Charlton Mariette, I really couldn't. Much as I'd like to. It's just not possible.
Pop Montgomery, start pouring the port. Give the general his first. What colour, General? White, red, or mixed?

Brigadier I think, if you don't mind, red.
Pop Red for the General. Mixed for me. Red for you, Charley boy?
Mr Charlton I — I — I ...

Suddenly Pop stops, knife and steel poised in air

Pop God God. What a fool I am. I forgot.
Mariette Forgot what?
Pop What the General come to see me about. (*He lifts knife and steel excitedly in the air*)
Brigadier Oh! I forgot something too, Larkin. Stupid of me. I know Edith Pilchester will want to come and see you about the arrangements. That's her pigeon. She's a great organizer.
Pop Good old Edith. I love Edith. I kissed her once at a Christmas social. Don't think she ever forgot it.
Brigadier Could we arrange an evening for her to come? Say Friday?
Pop Friday it is.
Mariette (*sharply*) Pop, what was it you forgot?
Pop (*once more triumphantly brandishing the knife and steel*) Kids, we're going to hold the village gymkhana here! In our medder!

Mariette, in intense excitement, drops everything

Mariette Oh! Lovely, lovely man!

She rushes over to her father, embraces him passionately and covers him with kisses

Oh! Lovely, lovely Pop!
Pop You should really thank the General.
Mariette Oh! thank you, thank you, General. Wonderful man!

She kisses the Brigadier too, with vigour. The Brigadier beams, not at all displeased

Oh! it's marvellous! I feel like kissing everybody.

Mr Charlton looks apprehensive. Suddenly he realizes it may be his turn

I think I'll even kiss Charley.

It is. With a rush of excitement, fondness and all the rest of the uninhibited Larkin emotions, Mariette runs to Mr Charlton and gives him the most prolonged and passionate kiss of all. Mr Charlton offers no resistance. The kiss goes on for some moments

Ma appears bearing two succulent brown roast geese on a tray

Ma Here you are! Done to a turn!
Mariette How are you feeling now?
Mr Charlton A little more perfick.
Mariette That's more like it.
Pop (*sharpening his knife*) Now, Charley, leg or breast?

Curtain

ACT II

The same. Early evening on the following Friday

The weather is still very hot. When the CURTAIN *rises, Pop sits in the yard in his shirt-sleeves, drinking a Dragon's Blood and reading the* Beano. *Ma is inside the house preparing the evening meal*

Pop This hot wevver gives me a throat like a starfish. (*He glances at his glass, discovers that it is practically empty and drains it before getting up and going into the house for another beer*) Good day in the strawberry field, Ma? (*He goes to the Frigidaire and helps himself to the beer*)

Ma Lovely.

Pop How much you knock up today?

Ma Well, the kids haven't got home yet. Mariette's drivin' 'em back. But I daresay it'll be on the shiny side of fifteen quid.

Pop What about Charley?

Ma Reckon he's got more money in his pocket than he's ever seen. You have a good day?

Pop Perfick. Nice little deal in scrap. Not very big, mind you, but showed about six hundred per cent. Wurfwhile. Cheers, Ma.

Ma Cheers what with? What about the old cook again?

Pop Sorry, Ma. What'll it be?

Ma What was that you mixed me last night? That was nice.

Pop My latest. Special request of Charley's. The Mariette. Gin and pineapple, dash of angostura and plenty of ice. Like that?

Ma Please. Just what I fancy.

He starts to prepare Ma's drink

Pop Bumped into Sir George Bluff-Gore in *The Saracen's Head* at lunch-time.

Ma What did he have to say?

Pop Not much. Looked about as cheerful as a pall-bearer with indigestion, as usual. I didn't do him no good neither.

Ma Oh?

Pop Offered him five thousand to sell Gore Court.

Ma Not for us to live in?
Pop Not likely.
Ma What did he say?
Pop Just laughed. Have to come to it, though, I told him. Ridiculous. Sixty
rooms, acres of farms, dairies and stables with nothing in 'em, half a mile
of greenhouses, an orangery with no oranges in it, everything gone to pot,
hundred tons of coal to keep the place lukewarm in winter and him and
Lady Rose living in a converted cowshed at the back. Toffs make you laugh
sometimes, don't they, Ma? Don't have no fun at all. (*He brings the drink
to Ma*) Reminds me.

He seizes Ma in an expert embrace and kisses her with prolonged passion

Just felt like it. Must be the smell of food.

He starts to embrace her a second time

Ma You know what I always tell you? If I'm to get the dinner I've no time
to lark around with you. Which do you want most — me or your food?
Pop Both.
Ma You'd better save it for Edith Pilchester. She'll be here in a minute.
Pop Of course, coming to talk about the gymkhana. Edith's all right. I like
Edith. Not like George Carter and Jack Woodley and a few other local
baskets I could name.
Ma Freda O'Connor and Molly Borden for two.
Pop Sent the General along as their messenger-boy 'cos they wouldn't lower
themselves to speak to the likes of us.
Ma That's their problem. But I like the General. He might not live very grand
but he's unmistakably a gent. And I like Edith.
Pop Edith's a sport.
Ma I daresay. But don't you get taking her up in the bluebell wood when
you've finished running your eye over that meadow. I don't know though
— might do her good. Expect she'd sleep sweeter. Trouble with you,
though, you don't know your own strength.
Pop Hot weather, that's what it is. I wonder how it affects 'em in real hot
countries?
Ma (*drily*) I wonder.
Pop Hullo: here comes Edith now.

*Edith Pilchester appears in the yard. She is about forty-five, sallow, heavy-
featured, rather hearty. In spite of the hot evening she is wearing a thick
cabbage-green thorn-proof skirt and a cable-stitch cardigan to match*

Pop, drink in hand, goes out to meet her

Miss Pilchester Oh! isn't it absolutely ghastly?
Pop What?
Miss Pilchester This heat. This weather.

Pop laughs in his customary ringing fashion

Pop Thought for a minute you meant my Rolls standing out there in the yard.
Miss Pilchester So it *is* yours? I must confess that when I saw it I said to
myself it couldn't be yours. Sorry. Was that absolutely ghastly?

*Miss Pilchester darts quick, nervous swallow-like glances at Pop almost
each time she speaks to him*

Pop What about a wet, Edith? Drop o' gin? Drop o' Guinness? Glass o' beer?
Cocktail? Dragon's Blood?
Miss Pilchester Would it be absolutely ghastly to say I preferred whisky?
A teeny-weeny drop.
Pop Anything you like. Ma's got gin and pineapple. Or would you rather
have a Red Bull? That's a blinder, that'll grow hair.
Miss Pilchester Oh, good-evening, Mrs Larkin. I'm sorry. I was busy
talking to your husband I didn't see you there. No, really, whisky please.

*Pop goes into the house to get the whisky. Miss Pilchester comes to the door
and talks to Ma*

I must say he's been an absolute Trojan about this meadow. Don't know
what we'd have done without him. The whole thing would have been a
complete shambles. Absolutely ghastly.
Ma He loves doing it. For Mariette's sake if nothing else.
Miss Pilchester I saw her out riding the other day. She looks so sweet and
trim and modest on a horse. I envy her.
Ma You do? Well, excuse me, Miss Pilchester, we killed a pig the day before
yesterday. The pork's just come home from the bacon factory and I must
get it into the deep-freeze.
Pop Save a nice cut for Edith, Ma. And a bit o' liver and a few chitterlings.

Ma goes

Like chitterlings, Edith? Well, here's your whisky anyhow.

*If Miss Pilchester is taken back by the remark about chitterlings she is even
more taken back by the size of the drink Pop has brought her. It almost fills
a tumbler*

Cheers. Here's to the gymkhana.

Miss Pilchester Cheers. And again many, many, many thanks for getting us out of this ghastly hole.

Miss Pilchester indulges in more swallow-like glances at Pop

Pop Pleasure. We've been talking a lot about this gymkhana. Decided to have a cocktail party after it's all over.
Miss Pilchester You? A cocktail party?
Pop It's the done thing nowadays. Everybody has cocktail parties. You'll come, won't you? You'll get a proper invite later.
Miss Pilchester Absolutely adore it.
Pop Sit down. Take the load off your feet. I'll get a chair. (*He gets a chair from the house. He sets it in the yard for Miss Pilchester, then finds a box for himself to sit on. He puts this quite close to the chair*) Going to have champagne.
Miss Pilchester Not at our gymkhana?
Pop No, no. At the party.

Miss Pilchester laughs nervously

Miss Pilchester Ghastly fool I am. For one awful second I could see the Pony Club funds going down the drain.
Pop No, no, no. Anythink extra I pay for. Fireworks, for instance — fireworks are on me.
Miss Pilchester Fireworks? What fireworks?
Pop Must have fireworks. Must have a few bangers.
Miss Pilchester No fireworks.
Pop Good God, Edith, why not?
Miss Pilchester No fireworks where there are animals. It would be absolutely ghastly.
Pop All right. Afterwards. At the party.
Miss Pilchester If you don't mind — not even at the party. There may still be some animals that have not been taken home and you never know.
Pop Just a few.

He begins to stroke Miss Pilchester's knee. She palpitates with pleasure

Miss Pilchester Not even a few.
Pop Just one, then. I promise not to let it off under you, Edith.

He caresses Miss Pilchester's knee with smoother determination

Miss Pilchester No. Not even if you promise. Furthermore I believe you're trying to be very naughty.

Pop All right. No fireworks.
Miss Pilchester Promise?
Pop Promise.
Miss Pilchester Good boy. (*She laughs nervously*). Sorry, that must have sounded absolutely ——
Pop On one condition.
Miss Pilchester What condition?
Pop You ride in the Ladies' Donkey Derby.
Miss Pilchester Oh! I absolutely couldn't ——
Pop I saw one once on television. Lot o' fun. Did you see it on television?
Miss Pilchester I have no television. I couldn't possibly afford one.
Pop No television? Terrible. You'll love the Donkey Derby. Hell of a lark.
Miss Pilchester I couldn't possibly sit on a donkey. They're so hairy.

Pop caresses Miss Pilchester's knee with still firmer purpose

Pop Edith, do you remember that Christmas? At the village hall?
Miss Pilchester Am I ever likely to forget it?
Pop How about another one like that?

Before Miss Pilchester can object Pop seizes her in an expert embrace and starts to kiss her with velvety passion. After a few seconds he breaks off

Miss Pilchester What is it? There's no-one about, is there?
Pop You're not giving much.
Miss Pilchester (*desperately*) I was trying my hardest to give all I'd got.

Pop gets to his feet

Pop I think we'd better start playing double or quits.

Miss Pilchester also gets up, rather agitatedly

Miss Pilchester Oh, please.
Pop All right. Here we go. (*He suddenly stops in the act of embracing Miss Pilchester*). No we don't though. What about the Donkey Derby? Come on, Edith. You always were a sport.
Miss Pilchester (*desperately*) Who else will be riding?
Pop All girls of your age.
Miss Pilchester Now you're trying to be naughty again. Oh no, I couldn't. I couldn't possibly. They're absolutely ghastly, those creatures.
Pop Only one thing for that — wear cardboard drawers.
Miss Pilchester Oh! you wicked man!

She falls into Pop's arms in passionate surrender, giving all she has got. Pop seizes the opportunity with expert hands, kissing her with prolonged skill and fervour. Half-way through the kiss the sound of a truck pulling up across the yard is heard. This is followed by sound of doors banging and of voices. The kiss is still in progress when the Larkin children arrive

Primrose, Victoria, Montgomery and the twins come in. They are all carrying chip baskets of strawberries. They are also eating the strawberries, together with their customary ice-creams and potato crisps

The sight of Pop kissing Miss Pilchester has no visible effect on them at all. They simply go straight into the house and sit down, as usual, in front of the television. Their only reaction is to say a brief "hullo" to Pop as they pass him

Montgomery
Zinnia } (*together*) Hullo, Pop. Hullo, Miss Pilchester.
Petunia

Mariette comes in, also carrying a basket of strawberries

Mariette Hullo, Pop. Had a good day? Just going upstairs to get a shower. Have a strawberry.

She sets the basket down on a box and then she too goes into the house and disappears

The kiss comes to an end. Miss Pilchester appears to be in a state of palpitating, ecstatic exhaustion

Miss Pilchester Don't you think we'd better go to the meadow now?
Pop Good idea.

Miss Pilchester, in a state of flux, prepares to go. She almost clutches at air

Pop Don't go without finishing your drink up. You may be glad o' that.
Miss Pilchester Yes, I certainly may. (*She finishes up her drink in a series of gulps which in turn register ecstasy, bewilderment, uncertainty, pleasure and even despair*)
Pop Take one with us, shall we?
Miss Pilchester No thanks. Enough is as good as a feast.

Miss Pilchester and Pop start walking across the yard. Miss Pilchester stops

There was just one more thing — something I wanted to ask you. Do you think all governments are dishonest?

Pop Course I do. Why?

Miss Pilchester A year or two ago I bought three and a half per cent War Stock at ninety-six and now I see from *The Times* this morning that it's down to sixty-seven. Don't you think that's dishonest? Isn't that an absolute swindle? Isn't that absolutely ghastly?

Pop Cruel. What did you say you saw that in?

Miss Pilchester *The Times.*

Pop Never heard of it.

Miss Pilchester I'm sure they're *all* dishonest — the governments, I mean, not *The Times*. All they think about is robbing you of every penny you've got. What do you think? You're so clever about money.

Pop What do I think? I think you want to rob them afore they get a chance of robbing you.

Miss Pilchester I hope you didn't mind my asking. (*She clutches Pop's arm impulsively, squeezing it.*) You've been an absolute lamb.

Pop Think nothing of it. Hullo, clap hands. Here comes Charley.

Mr Charlton enters. He presents a surprising figure. He is bare to the waist, except for a sweat-handkerchief tied round his neck. His face, arms and torso are a rich, fiery brown. Ten hours a day in the strawberry field, under a hot sun, for nearly a week, have made him a new man. He is actually whistling as he swings his basket of strawberries

How goes it, Charley boy? Had a good day?

Mr Charlton Splendid. Terribly hot, though. Mind if I help myself to a beer? (*He sets his basket of strawberries down on the ground*)

Pop Anything you want. By the way, this is Miss Pilchester. You remember, she's running the gymkhana. Edith — a friend of ours, Mr Charlton. Mr Charlton's on sick leave. He's organizing the cocktail party. Knows all about what you eat at cocktail parties and all that lark.

Miss Pilchester How do you do.

Mr Charlton Good-evening, Miss Pilchester.

They shake hands. Miss Pilchester casts him one or two of her swallow-like glances

Miss Pilchester Heavens, how brown you are.

Her admiring eyes follow him as he goes towards the house. At the door he stops and turns

Mr Charlton I heard it was the hottest day for seventy years today. So hot in the strawberry field everybody stripped down to their underwear.
Pop Wimmin too?
Mr Charlton (*nodding*) Electrifying sight.

He goes into the house. Pop and Miss Pilchester cross the yard. Just before disappearing Pop stops and looks back in the direction of Mr Charlton

Pop Wonderful what hot weather'll do.

Pop and Miss Pilchester depart

Mr Charlton appears at the door of the house with a large mug of beer. He drinks deeply and, with a certain swagger, wipes his mouth on the back of his hand

Mr Charlton Ah!

He actually belches. Suddenly the noise of a motor scooter is heard off stage. Its brakes squeak sharply as it draws to a standstill across the yard

A moment later Pauline Jackson enters. She is a big, well-made, sun-burned, blonde of nineteen, with a deeply sculptured bosom, and sleeveless black sweater, tight black jeans and large blue eyes. Her hair is done up in a pony tail

Pauline Hullo. Ready? I thought you were going to meet me on the corner?
Mr Charlton Just had to have a drink. I was so hot.
Pauline A swim will cool you down.
Mr Charlton It's awfully kind of you to give me a ride on your Vespa, Miss Jackson.
Pauline Pleasure.
Mr Charlton I've been trying to get into town all week to pick up a change of clothes at my lodgings. But you know how it is — time slips by so fast ——
Pauline Does it? Suppose it does. Depends who you're with ——

By now she has sidled up close to him. She puts her bare arm against one of his, comparing it

You're nearly as brown as I am. You tan easily, don't you? Like me.

Mr Charlton, although under a spell, is a little uncertain of this behaviour going on so close to the house and he backs slightly away

The first day you were in the strawberry field you were so pale, I couldn't
take my eyes off you.

Mr Charlton You mean you actually saw me that first day?

Pauline Of course I did. Couldn't help it. Everybody was talking about you.
(*She smiles seductively. For the third or fourth time*) Shall we go? I'm
longing for the feel of cool water on my body. Aren't you?

Mr Charlton Well, I — just hang on a moment, will you, while I get a shirt
— only a moment — I'll be straight back ——

*In his old nervous uncertain way Mr Charlton backs into the house and
disappears*

*When he has gone Pauline sidles over to where the baskets of strawberries
have been left. Idly, with languid movements of her splendid body, she picks
up a basket and from it takes a strawberry. She eats it with lips that move
lusciously. She picks out a second strawberry*

   Mariette comes to the door

Mariette Oh, I see we have company.

Pauline Cedric has company, if that's what you mean.

Mariette So it's Cedric, is it?

Pauline And why not?

The two girls eye each other up and down with calm scorn   ·

Mariette Just visiting? Or going somewhere?

Pauline For a swim. At the pool.

Mariette Really? I didn't know you washed.

Pauline Strawberry?

*She holds the basket out, but Mariette ignores it. Pauline chooses another
strawberry with elaborate care*

Mariette I often wondered why you wear black so much. Suits you I
suppose.

Pauline They tell me it does.

Mariette And is Cedric coming to the pool too?

Pauline That's what we arranged.

Mariette Very nice.

Pauline Sure you won't have a strawberry?

Again she holds out the basket and again Mariette ignores it

Seem extra good this year. Bigger and sweeter.

She starts to bite on another strawberry. The tension between the girls increases, though their voices still remain merely sarcastic and calm

Mariette Looks small and tart to me.
Pauline I wouldn't know. Sure you won't have just one strawberry?

She holds out one berry, mockingly. This is too much. With a scream of rage Mariette dashes at Pauline

Mariette Why don't you ruddy well go somewhere else and eat your own bloody strawberries?

A second later the two girls are locked in screaming, raging combat, pulling hair, tearing clothes, throwing strawberries and rubbing strawberries into each other's faces. Occasionally they knock each other down and maul on the ground. The fight attracts the rest of the family. First the children leave their television set and come into the yard laughing and shouting encouragement to Mariette

Ma also appears. She is knitting and her completely unruffled pose as she leans against the door post with her needles, watching the fight, is typical

Soon the girls are spitting and screeching. They fight like wild cats. Mariette, urged on by the family, gets slightly the better of the combat

Mr Charlton appears, still hastily putting on his shirt. He gets no further than the door, where he stands in shocked bewilderment, baffled not so much by the screaming, fighting girls as by Ma's pose of bland, unruffled calm

He addresses a question to Ma, but no-one can hear it and Ma merely shrugs her shoulder in answer. Suddenly Pauline, torn, dishevelled, half-weeping and crimson with strawberry stains, is in retreat. Mariette, looking very little better, pursues her

Pauline runs off stage

Mariette stands screaming after her

From the opposite side of the yard a figure even more bewildered than Mr Charlton appears. It is the Tax Inspector

Slut! Tart! Trollop! Baggage! Bitch! ——— (*She starts to take off her shoes. In rage she throws one after Pauline*) And you're no virgin either! (*She throws the other shoe*)

The effect of her final words is to petrify the Tax Inspector, who stands stock-still, simply staring, and further to shock Mr Charlton. The Vespa starts up and roars away and Mariette, now in full sail, turns and shouts at Mr Charlton

I'll be in the bluebell wood if you want me! That's where I'll be! Unless you'd rather go and help wash her filthy neck in the pool!

She flounces out — proud, dishevelled and victorious

Mr Charlton, shocked and aghast, takes a moment or two to recover

Mr Charlton But that was terrible. Terrible. What on earth were they fighting for?
Ma Gorblimey, don't you know?

All the Larkin children roar with laughter as they troop back into the house to resume watching television

Mr Charlton But she hasn't got her shoes on. She'll cut her feet. She hasn't got her shoes.
Ma (*still knitting as calmly as ever*) Then you'd better take them after her, hadn't you?

Without a word, Mr Charlton crosses the yard to go after Mariette. Absorbed in this pursuit he passes the Tax Inspector on the way

Inspector Good-evening.
Mr Charlton Good-evening.

Mr Charlton vanishes, shirt tails still hanging out, without a sign of recognition

The Tax Inspector stops and stares after him. He shakes his head

Inspector Can't be. Can't be.

He stares again after the transformed and unrecognizable Mr Charlton and again shakes his head. Ma stirs at the doorway and, still knitting, comes to meet him

Couldn't be. Couldn't be.
Ma Hullo, come to fetch your geese? I'll get them. They're all ready.

Ma goes into the house

The Tax Inspector stands in the yard, staring back in the direction of Mr Charlton

Inspector It couldn't be. Never in a million years. Could it?

CURTAIN

SCENE 2

The same. Three weeks later. Evening

The Larkins' cocktail party has begun. A babble of voices from inside the house indicates that it is full to overflowing. The overflow includes Miss Pilchester and the Brigadier, Sir George and Lady Bluff-Gore, Mariette and Mr Charlton, Ma and Pop

As the CURTAIN *rises the twins are just finishing nailing a notice to the doorframe of the house. It says* LADIES UPSTAIRS. *Having finished, they go into the house and return a few moments later with plates of tit-bits, which they hand round before disappearing. At the same time Montgomery and Pop see that champagne glasses are kept filled*

Charley leads Mariette by the hand across the yard and indicates for her to sit on a sawing-horse away from the throng. He clearly has something on his mind and begins to talk earnestly to her. During the following party dialogue we see she is responding warmly to his overtures. Eventually Charley goes down on one knee before her and obviously proposes marriage. A delighted Mariette takes his face in her hands and kisses him gently

Pop More champagne, Ma?
Ma Lovely.

She holds out her glass and Pop fills it

Pop Good idea of Charley's, this — having champagne. Perfick. Makes it easier for filling up.
Ma Like Mariette says, something extra nice always happens when you have champagne.
Pop Think everybody's enjoying theirselves?
Ma Own fault if they're not.

There is a loud cackle of laughter from Edith Pilchester, who is talking to the Brigadier

Pop Edith's off. By the way, Ma, how many people did we invite to this lark?
Ma Oh! about twenty-odd. Apart from ourselves.
Pop Lot o' people I never even seen before.
Ma Oh! Charley says that's always the way at cocktail parties. You got to be prepared for a lot of strangers.

The Tax Inspector comes into the yard. He is carrying a glass of champagne and munching on a biscuit. He looks carefully this way and that

Pop That's what I mean. Who's he?
Ma Never seen him before.
Pop Face looks a bit familiar.
Ma Must be one of the judges from the gymkhana.
Pop Could be, I suppose.

As the Inspector of Taxes walks slowly towards the house, he fails to notice Charley and Mariette. However Charley sees him and becomes more agitated in what he is saying to Mariette. The Inspector is about to go into the house when the Brigadier takes him by the arm. They greet each other. The Brigadier, in introducing him to Edith Pilchester, makes a remark which causes Edith to laugh aloud again

Ma Edith's certainly enjoying herself. By the way, have you kissed her lately?
Pop Not since that night she came up to look at the medder. You remember, I gave her an extra one for luck.
Ma Soon be time she had her ration again, won't it?
Pop Suppose so. I promised her one anyway if she went in for the Donkey Derby.
Ma Well, never break a promise. What's it like anyway?
Pop What's what like?
Ma The sensation.
Pop Oh that. (*He laughs*) Hard to say. You feel her teeth are going to crack like walnuts under the strain. She hangs on like a starving ferret.
Ma (*laughing like a jelly*). Wonder what it feels like to her? Ah well, does her good. Makes her sleep all the sweeter. Bit of comfort for her. Hasn't had much in her time, I'll bet. Hullo, she looks as if she's coming over. I'll leave you. Don't squeeze her any harder than you would me.
Pop You head her off! I want to talk to Sir George.

Pop seeks out Sir George: Ma arranges for Miss Pilchester to talk with Lady Bluff-Gore. While this re-arrangement is taking place, Charley and Mariette break from their embrace and look around for Pop who is taking Sir George aside. Sir George is cadaverous, humourless and funereal. Pop slaps him on the shoulder. He recoils with considerable distaste

Meanwhile, the Inspector of Taxes goes into the house and disappears

Having a good time, Sir George? Enjoy the gymkhana? What about the Donkey Derby, old man? Bit of a lark, eh? Livened things up. Perfick. I always say these gymkhanas want livening up a bit.

Sir George Yes.

Pop Too much solemn-eye about a lot of it. Fond mammas gnashing teeth because little Trixie didn't win the trot and canter — by the way, where's your daughter tonight? Not here?

Sir George Lives in London now. Chelsea.

Pop Working?

Sir George Gone over to art.

Pop Art? Who's he?

Sir George Wants to be a painter. Dreadful affair.

Pop Oh! I get you. By the way ——

An agitated Mr Charlton and Mariette come up and break in on the conversation

Mariette Pop, could you spare a minute? Charley has something terribly important he wants to ask you.

Pop Not now, not now. I'm talking business with Sir George.

Mr Charlton Pop ——

Mariette It's terribly important.

Mr Charlton Mr Larkin ——

Pop In a minute, in a minute ——

Mr Charlton Sir ——

Mariette Charley may have to leave in a moment, Pop.

Pop Leave? What's he want to leave for, in the middle of the party?

Mr Charlton Something important has cropped up.

The Inspector of Taxes reappears in the house, some yards from the threshold

The sight is too much for Mr Charlton

Oh! My God.

Mr Charlton turns and vanishes in the opposite direction like an eel

Mariette Pop, do listen to him. He's been trying to say something to you all evening and he can never get you alone. Please, Pop, please. Just listen for a minute. For just one minute. He may have to go.

Pop Go? He's already gone.

Mariette Oh! my lord. Charley, where are you? Charley!

She turns and rushes after Charley, who has long since disappeared in the direction of the woods. After a significant pause, the Inspector follows

Sir George Who is that young man? He seems unusually excited.

Pop Young friend of ours. Staying with us on sick leave. Here, did he call me sir?

Sir George Rather fancy he did.

Pop Can't feel well. Too much champagne, I expect.

Sir George Probably wants to borrow some money.

Pop Think so? Well, as long as it's nothing serious. Cigar?

Sir George Given up smoking. Can't afford it. Iniquitous price. Either that or whisky. Couldn't give up both.

Pop Don't mind if I do?

Pop starts to light his cigar. Puffing smoke, he taps Sir George on the shoulder and addresses him fraternally

Sir George, what about that little suggestion I made the other day? You know, about selling Gore Court?

Sir George Unthinkable, man.

Pop Cash. Ready as Freddy. Tax free.

Sir George Unthinkable I tell you. Out of the question.

Pop But you don't live in the damn thing.

Sir George That, Larkin, is hardly the point.

Pop Like having a television set you never look at.

Sir George (*with acid severity*) I have no television set.

Pop Tell you what. I'll go up five hundred.

Sir George Quite unthinkable.

Pop I'll make it nine thousand. At the present rate of tax that's equal to about — well, I dunno — about a hundred thousand.

Sir George (*severely*) Larkin. Setting aside the fact that I do not wish, have no intention of and am not considering selling Gore Court at any price, what, may I ask, would *you* do with it if you had it?

Pop Pull the ruddy thing down.

Sir George Good God. (*He remains speechless for some seconds*) I was born in that house. I think I will have that cigar after all. Thank you.

Pop (*whipping out the cigar case*) Course. Have a couple.

With frigid dignity Sir George selects a cigar. He then puts it to his nose

Sir George Havana, eh? (*He savours its fragrance*)

   Mariette and Charley rush past and into the house. They are no sooner in than they are out again and away towards the woods

   Larkin, do you know what I think? I think that young man is trying to elope with your daughter.
Pop Wouldn't put it past him.
Sir George Extraordinary behaviour.
Pop Couldn't say boo to a goose when he first came here. That reminds me. Can I send you up a couple o' geese for Sunday, old man? Got some nice young fat ones. No trouble. Ready plucked ——
Miss Pilchester Oh! There you are. I've been trying to get near you all evening.

With the rapturous arrival of Miss Pilchester, Sir George's obligations are temporarily over and he departs

   What a heavenly day. Have you ever walked on air?
Pop Eh!
Miss Pilchester I thought you must have. You're so lyrical sometimes.
Pop Me?
Miss Pilchester Do you remember that night when I came to look at the meadow? You were awfully lyrical then.
Pop No?
Miss Pilchester Frightfully. The cuckoo was calling. You asked me to listen. It reminded me of that wonderful line — "Oh! cuckoo shall I call thee bird or but a wandering voice?"
Pop Did it? Here, I'll mix you a Red Bull. You'll feel better.

The Inspector appears again from the direction of the woods, still on the prowl

Pop spots him and seizes a chance to change the subject

   By the way, who is that feller? You were talking to him with the Brigadier.
Miss Pilchester (*indifferently*). Oh! his name's Gorridge or something like that. He's something to do with Customs and Excise. Inland Revenue or whatever.
Pop Inland Revenue? Here, I got to go. I got to find Ma ——
Miss Pilchester No, you don't. You still haven't kept your promise. (*She gazes up at him in enraptured silence*) I'm ready when you are.

Pop What? In the middle of the party?
Miss Pilchester (*softly*) Come over here.

She takes Pop's hand and they move away

And in case I don't get another chance of talking to you alone again, thanks for everything. Heavenly, wonderful day. Best gymkhana we ever had. All your doing. And this party. Oh! I'm so frightfully, frightfully happy.

She falls with passionate abandon into Pop's arms. Pop, after a quick look round, kisses her with his usual prolonged velvety passion

In the middle of it all Ma appears in the yard with a tray of cocktail snippets. She pauses and looks on at the passionate performance for a moment or two with utter unconcern. Then she makes as if to offer Pop and Miss Pilchester the tray, thinks better of it, takes a couple of snippets herself and goes back into the house

No sooner has she gone than Miss Pilchester, with a despairing sob of ecstasy, breaks from Pop's embrace and rushes into the house. As she does so she almost runs into Angela Snow. She is tall, aristocratic, very fair and with a figure like a reed. Her long primrose dress makes her a most cool, attractive, languid creature. Her voice drawls delightfully. Surprised at Miss Pilchester's undue haste, she pauses, looks after her and then up at the sign LADIES UPSTAIRS. From this she draws the obvious conclusions. Turning back towards the yard she bumps into the Tax Inspector, also in a hurry

Angela Snow Must be the champagne.
Inspector I beg your pardon?
Angela Snow Nothing. You seem to be in a hurry, that's all. Looking for something?
Inspector I suppose you haven't by any chance seen a young man named Charlton here?
Angela Snow Never heard of him, honey. I'm a stranger here too.
Inspector Excuse me.

The Inspector goes into the house and disappears

Angela Snow comes languidly into the yard and greets the Brigadier

Angela Snow Brigadier. My sweet.
Brigadier Angela. What a charming surprise!

She allows herself to be kissed on both cheeks

Angela Snow Lambkin. Lovely to see you. (*She glances round at the party*) Lovely party. Going like a bomb. But then it would, wouldn't it, with that man in charge?
Brigadier Larkin, you mean? Just going into the house.

Angela Snow turns to see Pop going into the house. With a languid smile she stares after him

  Pop disappears

She turns to carry on her conversation with the Brigadier as Ma comes out into the yard

  Mariette and Mr Charlton appear and waylay Ma

Mariette Ma, where's Pop? We can't find him anywhere.
Ma Just gone into the house. Be back in a minute, I expect.
Mariette We haven't been able to get near him all evening. What do you think he'll say, Ma?
Mr Charlton *Do* you think he'll say yes, Mrs Larkin?
Ma I should think so. Why not? Every reason to.
Mariette Come on, let's get him before we lose him again.

They turn away, only to turn back to Ma again as Mariette thinks of something

  In this second or two Pop appears

He is waylaid by Angela Snow as he gets to the doorway

Mariette Ma, perhaps you'd ask him instead, would you?
Ma Mr Charlton must ask him. It's Mr Charlton's business, not mine.

Charley and Mariette turn to approach Pop. They are out of luck again. Angela Snow is already there and Charley bumps straight into her

Mr Charlton So sorry. Oh! God, this is worse than tooth-ache.

He turns sharply, dragging Mariette away towards the house

Angela Snow (*greeting Pop*) Hullo, there. Going to buttonhole you for a moment if I may. (*She lays a long, cool, languid arm on one of Pop's*) Angela Snow, Emhurst Valley.

Pop How d'ye do.

Angela Snow Lovely to meet you. By the way, who was the pretty gel?

Pop My eldest daughter. Mariette.

Angela Snow Thought so. Powerful family likeness. And the bronzed young man?

Pop Oh! that's our friend Charley. Mr Charlton.

Angela Snow Really? Met a character just now who was looking for him. Tallish man.

Pop Inspector of Taxes.

Angela Snow You don't say? You mean the poor boy hasn't coughed up or something?

Pop Worse than that. He's supposed to work for him.

Angela Snow Supposed?

Pop Well, Charley was very run down, so he took a little sick leave. Now the inspector's chasing him to get back to the office.

Angela Snow The dirty rat.

Pop Oh! Charley'll work it out. Enjoying the party?

Angela Snow Enormously. By the way, they tell me you practically organized that whole bun-fight this afternoon single-handed. Marvellous affair.

Pop Glad you liked it.

Angela Snow Going to have a party of my own next week. Say you'll come. Dancing and all that. Do you dance at all?

Pop Used to fling 'em up a bit at one time.

Angela Snow Scream. (*She laughs on delicious bell-like notes*) And that donkey derby, they tell me, was your idea. Blistering success.

Pop Must admit I thought it went off quite well.

Angela Snow Seven foolish virgins on seven foolish donkeys. Scream. Couldn't stop laughing. Practically needed changing.

Pop I always think these things want an extra bang putting into 'em somehow, don't you?

Angela Snow Couldn't agree more. They can be absolute stinkers, gymkhanas, don't you think? Absolute stinkers. But you thought of the virgins. (*She holds him with delightfully candid eyes*) After all there are so few left, aren't there?

Pop looks hastily round

Pop Mind if I ask you something?

Angela Snow Anything you like, dear man.

Pop Like fireworks?

Angela Snow Love 'em. Adore 'em.

Pop I think this party needs hotting up a bit. What about a drink first? (*He indicates his own*) One of these.

Angela Snow What exactly is that?
Pop One of my own. Red Bull. Hair curler.
Angela Snow Marvellous. Just what I need.
Pop This way.

Pop starts to take Angela Snow into the house. At the door he is waylaid by Mariette and Mr Charlton. At last they succeed in speaking to him

The Inspector enters the far side of the yard

Angela Snow goes to meet him

Angela Snow Hullo there. Still looking for your Mr Charlton?
Inspector I am. He's like the damned elusive Pimpernel.
Angela Snow He just went that way. (*She points in the opposite direction from the house*) Heard him say he was going to water the virgins' donkeys.
Inspector The *what*?
Angela Snow That way. *Do* hope you find him.

The Inspector departs

Angela Snow goes towards the house, where Pop is waiting for her. Just before she arrives, Mariette gives her father a passionately grateful hug and kiss and then drags Charley into the house

Angela Ah! there you are. Lead me to the hair-curlers, darling. I can't wait.

She takes Pop by the arm as if she has known him for years and they go into the house. Angels Snow's last remark is loud enough to be overheard by Ma and Lady Bluff-Gore. It quite startles Lady Bluff-Gore, but Ma is utterly unperturbed

Lady Bluff-Gore Extraordinary. Do you mind other women talking to your husband like that?
Ma Mind? I encourage it.
Lady Bluff-Gore Good gracious. Why?
Ma (*blandly*) Variety. Men like variety. Keeps 'em sweet.

Ma starts laughing in her usual jolly fashion and almost pokes Lady Bluff-Gore in the ribs

I lend him to Edith Pilchester sometimes. Keeps her sweet too. Sleeps like a top after it. Having a nice time?

Lady Bluff-Gore Charming, thank you. Such a lovely day. Such luck with the weather.

Ma Thought perhaps you might have gone in for that Donkey Lark, eh? Didn't fancy it?

Ma shrieks with laughter. Lady Bluff-Gore smiles, if a little frigidly

Lady Bluff-Gore Mrs Larkin, I hear that your husband has made a most extraordinary suggestion to Sir George. I've been trying to get hold of him all evening to talk to him about it. But he's so devastatingly popular.

Ma About pulling your house down?

Lady Bluff-Gore That's right.

Ma Just like Pop to say a thing like that. Afraid it must have shocked you.

Lady Bluff-Gore On the contrary, I've so often wanted to pull the bloody thing down myself.

The Brigadier walks across the yard with Sir George Bluff-Gore. The conversation between his wife and Ma ceases for a moment or two

Brigadier I've nothing to invest. Not a bean. I'm out of touch.

Sir George Disastrous.

Brigadier You see, it isn't as if the policy of one government differed from that of another. They all tread the same uniform, bare-faced, immoral primrose path of reckless rapacity — I've given it up. I've surrendered.

They go into the house. The conversation between Ma and Lady Bluff-Gore is resumed

Lady Bluff-Gore Of course my husband isn't the easiest of men.

Ma No, I suppose not.

Lady Bluff-Gore But it's not impossible to persuade him. Perhaps you'll give Mr Larkin a message for me?

Ma 'Course I will.

Lady Bluff-Gore Ask him to come and see me at eleven o'clock on Monday morning. Sir George will be in London. We could have a little talk together. I think we might even come to a little arrangement.

Ma I'll tell him. He'll be there.

Lady Bluff-Gore You know, all this has set me thinking. As a young woman I thought it would be marvellous to live in a mansion. Now I hate it. I almost envy you this place of yours — so tucked away from everywhere, with that bluebell wood and that lovely meadow — so quiet.

The first firework goes off with a terrific bang in the house. It is rapidly followed by other devastating explosions from all parts. Angela Snow runs

*from the house, laughing like a peal of bells and throws a firework into distant
junk. It goes off like a bomb. Pandemonium everywhere. Miss Pilchester runs
from the house, pursued by Pop*

*Miss Pilchester disappears off stage. Pop follows her and there is another
tremendous bang*

*After this more fireworks go off everywhere. Angela Snow goes back to the
house*

Mariette Where's Pop? We must find Pop. Ma, where has Pop gone?

Pop comes back

*He is at once waylaid by Mariette and Mr Charlton. Another devastating
bang goes off, just behind them*

Pop, listen, listen, listen, listen.

More bangs off stage

*Edith Pilchester runs across the yard, pursued by the twins, who are
waving sparklers. All three disappear into the house, from which there
comes another tremendous bang*

*In the pandemonium Mariette is seen stamping her foot in desperate appeal
to Pop*

Please, Pop. *Now!* Will you do it *now*?

*Pop makes a momentary escape and puts a firework under Ma. There is an
appalling bang. Ma does not move a muscle*

Pop Perfick!
Mariette Pop, *please*!

*The Inspector returns from his search and stands staring from the far side
of the yard*

*Mr Charlton is about to produce a chair for Pop to stand on when he is again
frozen by the sight of the Inspector. He knows that a showdown is coming and
is determined to stand his ground. By this time Pop is standing on a box in
the yard*

Pop Ladies and gentlemen, just a minute, your attention please. Gather round. Quiet! I got something to say.

Gradually order is restored. The guests and the children gather closely round. The only exceptions are the Inspector, who stands afar off, and Angela Snow, who keeps at a distance behind Pop

Ladies and gentlemen, friends, if I might just have your attention for a moment I've got an announcement I'd like to make. (*He laughs*) Ma ought to be doing this. She's better at it than me.
Ma Oh! spit it out, man, do.
Pop All right, all right.

The action now divides. On one side of the stage Pop gives a speech, which will end with the announcement of the engagement. On the opposite side of the stage Mr Charlton and the Inspector will come together for a test of strength that will culminate in the Inspector's realization when he hears of the engagement that Mr Charlton is lost for ever to the civilized world and he himself has no alternative but to retreat from the yard

(*Looking around*) Dear friends. Nigh on thirty years ago when I first came down to Kent with my mum and dad, my brother Perce, some cousins and a couple of aunts, I knew I was somewhere — somewhere very special. It was hop-picking time and the memory of it stayed with me all the following year until we come again. And it was like that every year until I was eighteen and then something else happened — something really special. I met a beautiful Kentish maid.

During this Mr Charlton has plucked up the courage to cross to the Inspector. Mariette is torn between joining him and staying close to Pop

Charlton Mr Gorridge.
Inspector Charlton. I thought it was you — first time I saw you — that Sunday when I needed water for the car.
Charlton Yes, it was me.
Inspector I must say you look remarkably well for a man who's on sick leave.
Charlton Oh! do I?
Inspector Remarkably. So well in fact, that I think it's time you came back to the office, don't you?
Charlton I — I ——
Pop *The Three Cocks* at Fordington. One or two of you may know it. Never been the same though since I persuaded the publican's daughter to run away with me to Brighton. Six children later she's still as lovely as ever.

Inspector Look at you, man. Your hair hasn't seen a comb in a week. Your face is all red and blotched. Most of your clothes look like hop-sacks. It's time to leave. Get your things.

Charlton It's not quite that simple, sir ——

Inspector Don't worry. I'll drive you back to your digs. Hot bath and a good night's sleep and you'll forget any of this ever happened.

Charlton I'm afraid not, sir. You see, I like it here.

Inspector You'll like it more on Monday morning when you've got your feet safely back under your office desk.

Charlton I'm not coming back. Not today, not Monday nor any other day.

Pop And so on this very happy evening I want to announce — (*To Mariette*) Where's Charley? I can't see Charley. (*Louder*) I want to announce ——

Mariette realizes she has to intervene. She crosses and takes Charley's hand and leads him back to stand by Pop. The Inspector looks on nonplussed

Mr Charlton Goodbye Mr Gorridge.

Pop Always the same these young 'uns. Never where you want 'em to be. Ah, there you are, Charley. Where you been?

Mr Charlton Sorry, Pop.

Pop Pop? I like that, Charley boy. Pop. All right — All right. Quiet now, ladies and gentlemen. It gives me great pleasure to announce ——

Angela Snow moves a little nearer to Pop

— to announce the engagement ——

Angela Snow bends down

— between Mr Cedric Charlton, better known as Charley, and my daughter Mariette.

As the guests cheer and clap and turn admiring and congratulatory glances on Mariette and Mr Charlton, Angela Snow walks away

I hope you all got your glasses filled? Perfick! All right, ladies and gentlemen, I give you the toast — Mariette and Charley ——

The most devastating bang of all goes off under Pop, blowing him backwards off the box. Everybody roars with laughter. Ma simply peals with delight

Ma One for his nob!

Mr Charlton Parson's Poke!

Mariette What Paddy shot at!

Angela Snow stands cool, serene and languid, admiring her handiwork

Angela Snow Absolutely perfick. You darling man.

Amid fresh excitement and laughter the Inspector, shaking his head in defeat, exits from the yard

Charley and Mariette hold hands watching him go

CURTAIN

SCENE 3

The same. Some time later that evening

When the CURTAIN *rises stars are shining and nightingales sing distantly in the woods. The party is over. The yard is deserted. Pop and Ma are alone in the house, sitting at the table. Ma is knitting serenely*

Pop I think we might say the party went off with a bang, Ma.
Ma Very nice. I enjoyed it.
Pop Ought to have one more often, I think, don't you?
Ma Good idea. By the way, who was that tall girl in the yellow dress. She was a spark.
Pop Friend of the General's.
Ma Gay spark.
Pop Her father's a judge, the General told me.
Ma Oh well, I suppose there's a throw-back in every family.

They sit quietly for a few moments

Pop Anythink left to eat, Ma? I'm feeling quite peckish.
Ma Think there's an apple tart in the fridge. I'll get it.

She puts her knitting on the table, goes to the fridge and comes back with an apple tart, a plate, a knife and a large bottle of tomato ketchup. She sets them all on the table and Pop cuts himself a slice of apple tart and starts to eat it

   Don't you want no ketchup?
Pop Gone off ketchup.

Ma Oh? How's that?
Pop Makes everything taste the same.
Ma Don't say you've gone off port too.
Pop No, no. Just got some more in. Get it in two-gallon jars now. Want a
drop?
Ma Please. (*She sits and starts knitting*)

*Pop goes out and comes back with a large wicker jar of port. He sets this
on the table and then goes to the cocktail cabinet to find glasses*

Oh! by the way, I've got a message for you.

Pop returns with the glasses

Pop Who from?
Ma Lady Bluff-Gore.
Pop Oh? (*He pours out two glasses of port.*)
Ma She heard about what you said to Sir George. About the house. About
pulling it down.
Pop Upset her?
Ma Don't think so. She said she longed for years to pull the bloody thing
down herself.

Pop roars with laughter

Pop She did, did she? Well, cheers, Ma. That's a good 'un, that is.
Ma She says will you go round and see her. Monday morning at eleven
o'clock.
Pop Why her?
Ma She said she thought you'd understand what a difficult man Sir George
was to persuade.
Pop About the house, you mean?
Ma I suppose so. Anyway she says she's got ways and means of doing it.
Pop What's she want to see me for?
Ma I fancy she thinks you and her could come to a little arrangement.

Pop laughs again

Pop Does she? Perfick. I always thought she'd got her head screwed on the
right way.
Ma Well, if she don't persuade him about the house you won't be able to pull
it down. So I suppose she's got a right to expect a drop o'cream off the top
o' the milk. That's only fair.

Pop Lady ten-per-cent, eh? (*He laughs quietly again*) Lady five-per-cent.

They sit for a few moments without speaking

Ma Edith enjoy herself tonight?
Pop Think so. Did my best for her.
Ma Saw her having a good cry once. Still, that'll do her good.
Pop Good as a dose o'medicine. By the way, did I make the announcement all right?
Ma Once you started to spit it out you did.

They sit quiet again

Pop By the way, Ma, I've been thinking.
Ma Steady now.
Pop Why don't you and me get married too?
Ma What made you think of that all of a sudden?
Pop Don't know. You ever thought of it?
Ma Now and then.
Pop Well, what about it?
Ma Might do. I've got to have my rings cut off again soon, they're starting to get so tight on my fingers. (*She calmly contemplates the many rings on her fat fingers*) Might be a good chance to do it then.
Pop We could make it a double wedding.
Ma Could do, I suppose.
Pop Anyway we could ask Mr Charlton what he thought.
Ma What's it got to do with Mr Charlton?
Pop He knows about everything. Look what he knew about the party — about the champagne and the hot bits of sardine on toast and all that. I give a lot o'marks to our Charley boy.
Ma I think he's been a big influence on our Mariette. I notice it more and more this last week or so.
Pop By the way, where are they?
Ma Having a quiet five minutes in the other room.
Pop I'll call 'em.
Ma No, not yet. Give 'em a chance. How would you like to be disturbed after you'd only been engaged a couple of hours?
Pop All right, Ma. Fair enough.
Ma He's got a lot of lost ground to make up, Charley has. He's got a lot to learn.
Pop Think he'll make a go of it?
Ma Oh I expect so. In time.
Pop I think he's got it in him, somehow, I do. He made a nice bit of underdone rump of that old inspector anyway.

Ma Yes, that was a welcome sight, that was. That was good. Oh! well, if he don't get on all that fast he'll have to take a few lessons from you, won't he?

Pop Who would you like me to demonstrate on?

Ma Edith if you like. I daresay Lady Bluff-Gore wouldn't say no either. She didn't half prick up her ears when I said I lent you out sometimes. (*She laughs resoundingly*)

Pop Here, steady on, Ma. You'll have me at stud next!

Ma That don't sound like you, somehow.

Pop Well, there's a limit, after all. I think I'll call Charley and Mariette. (*He gets up to go to the door and then, thinking of something, stops*) Here Ma, you're not in one of your primrose-and-bluebell moods are you?

Ma gives him a long, lustrous glance

Ma What do you expect after a nice party?

Pop I'm blowed if I didn't think so.

Pop comes back and seizes her deftly in the most obliterating and passionate of embraces, kissing her with prolonged fervour

Perfick, Ma. Absolutely perfick. I think we will get married after all.

Ma Wonder what it feels like to be married.

Pop Soon find out. Calls for another drink anyway. Champagne suit you?

Ma Lovely.

Pop Red or white?

Ma Red would make a change.

Pop starts to get glasses and a bottle of champagne. He also opens the door and calls across the passage

Pop Mariette. Charley. Come in here a minute. Got something to tell you.

Mariette and Charley presently appear

Pop has four glasses of champagne ready when they arrive

Mariette Ma, you haven't seen my ring.

Ma Duckie, that's a beauty.

Mariette holds out her left hand so that first Ma and then Pop can admire her engagement ring

Mariette It's a dream.

Ma suddenly hugs Mariette

Pop Perfick. What sort of stones?
Mariette Diamonds, rubies and — what were the others, sweetheart?
Mr Charlton Zircons.
Pop Never heard o'them.
Mr Charlton It's a rather uncommon stone. They're very fond of them in countries in the East.
Ma Oh duckie, it's marvellous.

Ma suddenly hugs Mr Charlton. Pop hugs Mariette and then shakes hands with Mr Charlton

Pop Well, here's to you both. Long life, 'elf and happiness. Gawd bless you.
Ma Bless you.

The four glasses are raised. They drink

Pop Well, Ma, shall we tell 'em our bit of news?
Ma You tell them.
Pop We're going to be married too.
Mariette Oh, lovely ——
Mr Charlton Now wait a minute. This wants thinking about.

Pop and Ma are stunned by his reaction

Pop What ——
Ma Why does it want thinking about?
Mr Charlton It would be fatal.
Ma ⎫
Pop ⎭ (*together*) Fatal?
Mr Charlton From the tax point of view, I mean. Don't you see, in your situation it's much better to go on living in ——
Ma (*sternly*) Living in what?
Mr Charlton I mean living as you are.
Ma I know what you were going to say. You were going to use that word, weren't you? I don't like that word.
Mr Charlton I'm sorry, Ma — I may call you Ma now, mayn't I? But ——
Mariette We could have a double wedding!
Mr Charlton No, no, no. It would be foolish.
Pop Well, that's a bit of a disappointment.
Mr Charlton As the law on tax stands it's better to go on living as single persons. It's greatly to your advantage to keep the *status quo*.
Pop Gorblimey. Status what?

Ma Quo?
Mr Charlton Stay as you are.
Ma It's quite a shock. Fancy not being able to get married when you want
to. With a big family like ours too.
Mr Charlton I don't say you can't. Don't think that. I merely say that's the
position. By all means get married if you want to. (*With sudden impulsive-
ness*) "Let me not to the marriage of true minds admit impediments ——"
Pop Eh?
Mariette Shakespeare! Charley recites it to me up in the bluebell wood.
(*Softly, with pride and tenderness*) "Love is not love which alters when it
alteration finds, or bends with the remover to remove ——"
Mr Charlton (*vehemently*) "Oh! no! it is an ever-fixed mark that looks on
tempests and is never shaken; it is the star to every wand'ring bark, whose
worth's unknown all though his height be taken."

Ma and Pop are open-mouthed, mute and stunned

Mariette I didn't make a single mistake, did I?
Mr Charlton You knew every word. You knew it all. Perfick. I mean —
perfect.
Pop Ma, I don't think you and me had better get married after all.
Ma I don't think so either. Better go on in the old sweet way.
Mr Charlton Splendid! I'm so glad. You see, by keeping to the old way
you'll be so much better off when the time comes.
Pop When the time comes for what?
Mr Charlton When the time comes to pay your tax. It's bound to catch up
with you one day.

Pop roars with laughter

Pop Hear that, Ma? Bound to catch up one day! That's what you think,
Charley.
Mr Charlton For instance, there's the Rolls Royce.
Ma What about the Rolls Royce?
Mr Charlton They'll want to know where the money came from.
Pop (*with scorn*) Money? That old crate? I took it for a debt!

He roars with laughter. Ma joins in

Oh! dear. Oh! dear, Charley, I thought you knew me better than that. And
you going to be my son-in-law. Anyway, if your boss sends anybody else
along with a tax form, I'll expect you to fill it in!

Mariette It's such a lovely night. Let's walk as far as the bluebell wood, shall we, and listen to the nightingales?
Ma That's it, duckie, you do that. Off you go.

Mariette and Mr Charlton start to move off

Pop Wait a minute. I just remembered something. I got a little proposition for you two.
Mariette What is it, Pop?
Pop If Lady Bluff-Gore and me come to a certain arrangement, I shall be pulling down Gore Court afore I'm many weeks older.
Mr Charlton Seems a shame.
Pop Some beautiful stuff in there. Mahogany staircase, lovely doors.
Ma If there's any nice pelmets, save them for me. Ever since I saw that programme on telly about that castle I wanted to have pelmets like that.
Pop Tell you what I thought I'd do, Charley boy. I'll pick out the plum stuff and build you and Mariette a bungalow in the medder, just by the side of the bluebell wood. How about that?
Mariette Oh! wonderful, wonderful Pop!

She impulsively kisses him then Ma and finally Mr Charlton

Isn't that wonderful? Charley?
Mr Charlton That would be very generous indeed.
Pop I think I'll have a cigar. What about you, Charley boy? You like a cigar?
Mr Charlton Thank you. (*He takes Pop's proffered cigar and lights it then he holds out his hand and shakes Pop's hand*) I just wanted to say, sir, how grateful I am. And how lucky.
Mariette Thank you, Pop. Thank you over and over and over again. (*She turns to Ma*) Don't go to bed yet, Ma; we won't be long.
Ma Don't hurry yourselves. We'll be here.
Mariette Lovely night. So warm. And millions of stars.

They go across the yard, hand in hand, and stop for a moment or two on the other side of it

Pop, you can hear the nightingales. You should come and hear them.
Pop We will.

Mariette and Mr Charlton disappear

Pop is in something of a dream too. Ma is placidly knitting again

Pop You're certainly right about our Mariette. You don't half see a change
in her. Shakespeare. Blimey ——

*As Ma goes on knitting, Pop walks across the yard. He stands there in silence
for some moments, contemplating the sky*

Mariette's certainly right, Ma. It's beautiful. Paradise, Ma. Paradise.

*He breathes the summer evening air with half-rapturous satisfaction and at
the same time moved by the realization that his daughter has grown up*

Sniff that air. Take a good deep breath o' that, Ma. What did Mr Charlton
say to that drink we gave him? Nectar. That's it, nectar.

*Ma drops her ball of wool. Rather absentmindedly Pop stoops, picks it up and
gives it back to her*

Ma Midsummer day tomorrow, Pop. Days seem to fly past, don't they?
Pop There's just one thing bothers me about them two. Has Charley found
out about Mariette? I mean about the baby?
Ma She's not going to have a baby now. False alarm.
Pop Oh! Jolly good. (*He stops suddenly*) No, it ain't though. I don't know
whether I like that. I feel quite disappointed.
Ma You do? Why?
Pop I was looking forward to having a baby about the place again. Yes, I'm
disappointed.
Ma I don't think you need worry your head about that.
Pop Oh! Why?

Ma, calm and wonderful as ever, knits on

Ma What do you think I'm knitting for?

For a moment Pop stands stupefied, then suddenly grasps what she means

Pop (*joyfully*) Oh, Ma! Perfick!!

The Lights slowly fade

CURTAIN

FURNITURE AND PROPERTY LIST

ACT I
SCENE 1

On stage: LIVING-ROOM/KITCHEN
1950s black and white television
Glass and chromium cocktail cabinet. *In it*: glasses, tumblers, 2 ice-
buckets, various bottles of gin, whisky, brandy, bitters, etc., cocktail
shaker. *Under it*: box of cigars, tray. *On top*: copy of "A Guide to
Better Drinking"
Sideboard. *In it*: knives, forks, spoons, carving knife and steel, table-
cloth, tray
French polished table
8 chairs
Radio
Pictures on wall
Curtains (open) at window
Waste-paper basket
New electric cooker (practical)
Large 1950s Frigidaire. *In it*: bottles of beer, jugs of cream, 3 eggs, plate
of sardines, block of strawberry mousse
Cupboards. *In them*: bottles of vinegar, Worcester sauce and tomato
ketchup, plates, cups, saucers, bowls, egg cups, saucepans, etc.
Work top. *On it*: bread, bread knife, butter in dish, kettle

YARD
Broken pig troughs
Old perambulators
Worn-out tyres
Sacks
Wheels
Boxes
Corrugated iron
Oil drum
Various other junk including old iron
Chestnut tree. *Hanging from it*: worn-out tyres

Off stage: Chocolate-vanilla-raspberry ice-creams, bags and trays of food items
including fish and chips, iced buns, 6 packet of crisps (**Pop, Ma,
Montgomery, Primrose, Victoria, Zinnia, Petunia**)
Black briefcase containing buff-yellow tax forms (**Mr Charlton**)

Large basket containing 3 fresh pineapples (**Mariette**)
Large black and white television set (**Montgomery** and **Primrose**)
3 fat dead geese (**Pop**)

Personal: **Pop**: roll of one hundred pound notes
Ma: large drop pearl ear-rings, turquoise rings, large wrist-watch
Mr Charlton: spectacles, fountain pen

SCENE 2

Strike: All items from table

Set: Glass of Guinness, 2 glasses of cider, pack of playing cards, cribbage
board and pegs on table
Ice cubes in Frigidaire

Off stage: Pair of bright flowered pyjamas (**Mariette**)

Personal: **Pop**: box of matches
Mr Charlton: spectacles

SCENE 3

Strike: All items from table

Check: Sufficient cutlery and glasses in sideboard and cocktail cabinet
Cocktail cabinet closed

Set: LIVING-ROOM/KITCHEN
2 roast geese in oven
Ice-cubes in Frigidaire
Tray by cooker
Saucepans on cooker
Various items of food on work top
2 bottles of port by cocktail cabinet

YARD
Table under chestnut tree. *On it*: copies of *News of the World* and
Sunday Express
Chairs

Off stage: Ice-creams, potato crisps, blocks of chocolate and raspberry mousse
(**Montgomery, Primrose, Victoria, Zinnia** and **Petunia**)

Personal: **Mr Charlton**: dark glasses

ACT II

Scene 1

Strike: LIVING-ROOM/KITCHEN
              All food items and saucepans from kitchen

              YARD
              Table and contents

Set: Beer and ice-cubes in Frigidaire
              Clean glasses in cocktail cabinet
              Almost-empty glass and copy of the *Beano* on oil drum in yard

Re-set: Chairs from yard in house

Check: Cocktail cabinet closed

Off stage: Ice-creams, potato crisps, chip baskets of strawberries (**Montgomery,**
                 Primrose, Victoria, Zinnia and **Petunia**)
              Basket of strawberries (**Mariette**)
              Basket of strawberries (**Mr Charlton**)
              Knitting (**Ma**)

Personal: **Mr Charlton**: spectacles

Scene 2

Strike: All baskets of strawberries
              Used glasses

Set: LADIES UPSTAIRS notice, nail and hammer (for **Zinnia** and **Petunia**)
              Plates and trays of cocktail party food in living-room
              Bottle of champagne
              Glasses for guests

Off stage: Glass of champagne, biscuit (**Tax Inspector**)
              Sparklers (**Zinnia** and **Petunia**)

Personal: **Mr Charlton**: spectacles
              Pop: cigars in cigar case, matches, "firework"
              Angela Snow: "firework"

SCENE 3

Strike: All party items from table

Set: Knitting on table
                 Apple tart in Frigidaire
                 Bottle of champagne in Frigidaire
                 4 champagne glasses in cocktail cabinet

Check: Cocktail cabinet closed

Off stage: Large wicker jar of port (**Pop**)

Personal: **Pop**: cigars in case, matches
                 Mr Charlton: spectacles
                 Mariette: engagement ring on finger

LIGHTING PLOT

Property fittings required: nil.
1 interior, 1 exterior setting.

ACT I, Scene 1 Afternoon

To open: Bright, hot sunshine effect in yard; general interior lighting in
living-room/kitchen area

Cue 1   The children switch on the television   (Page 2)
Fade up greenish flicker effect from television

Cue 2   **Pop**: "Give us a chance."   (Page 9)
Cut television flicker effect

Cue 3   **Montgomery** and **Primrose** switch on television   (Page 10)
Fade up greenish flicker effect from television

ACT I, Scene 2 Evening

To open: Sunny evening gradually fading to brilliant starry night effect
in yard; general interior lighting in living-room/kitchen
area with greenish flicker effect from television

Cue 4   **Ma** and **Pop** stand wondering   (Page 28)
Slow fade to black-out

ACT I, Scene 3 Morning

To open: Bright, hot sunshine effect in yard; general interior lighting in
living-room/kitchen area

No cues

ACT II, Scene 1 Evening

To open: Sunny early evening effect in yard; general interior lighting in
living-room/kitchen area

Cue 5   The children switch on the television   (Page 48)
             Fade up greenish flicker from television

ACT II, SCENE 2 Evening

To open: Sunny evening effect in yard; general interior lighting in
            living-room/kitchen area

No cues

ACT II, SCENE 3 Evening

To open: Brilliant starry night effect in yard; general interior lighting in
            living-room/kitchen area

Cue 6   **Pop**: "Oh, Ma! Perfick!!"   (Page 74)
             Fade to black-out

EFFECTS PLOT

ACT I

Cue 1   As the CURTAIN rises   (Page 1)
Farm animal sounds and birdsong in background, continue throughout scene; sound of truck drawing up, truck doors banging, followed by chorus of disturbed geese, ducks and hens in background

Cue 2   The children switch on the radio and television   (Page 2)
Snap on loud dance music from radio and fade up sound of television Western; fade radio after a while

Cue 3   **Mr Charlton** is about to hand Pop a form   (Page 6)
Alarming chorus of turkeys

Cue 4   **Mr Charlton:** "... what would you estimate ——"   (Page 9)
Volley of revolver shots from television

Cue 5   **Mr Charlton:** "Of course this is confidential ——"   (Page 9)
More revolver shots

Cue 6   **Montgomery** and Primrose change over the television set   (Page 10)
Cut television sound and then fade up again

Cue 7   To end SCENE 1   (Page 17)
Cut radio and television sound

Cue 8   **Pop** opens the cocktail cabinet   (Page 20)
Tune from the cocktail cabinet

Cue 9   To open SCENE 3   (Page 28)
Church bells ring in the distance

Cue 10   **Mr Charlton** is about to put the tray on the table   (Page 29)
Long, low distinguished honeyed sound of motor horn

Cue 11   **Mr Charlton** sets down the tray a second time   (Page 29)
Peremptory snarl of motor horn

Cue 12   **Mr Charlton** busies with the glass and cutlery   (Page 30)
2 motor horn sounds alternating every few seconds; then stops

Cue 13	**Mr Charlton** "I rather fancy he's just arrived." *2 motor horn sounds sounds*	(Page 30)
Cue 14	**Mr Charlton** retires *Repeat previous effect*	(Page 30)
Cue 15	**Pop**: "That's very bad." *Urgent snarl of motor horn*	(Page 31)
Cue 16	**Pop** opens the cocktail cabinet to mix the drinks *Tune from cocktail cabinet*	(Page 32)

ACT II

Cue 17	**Pop** opens cocktail cabinet to prepare **Ma's** drink *Tune from cocktail cabinet*	(Page 43)
Cue 18	**Pop** kisses **Miss Pilchester** *Sound of truck pulling up, truck doors banging*	(Page 48)
Cue 19	The children switch on the television *Fade up television sound*	(Page 48)
Cue 20	**Mr Charlton** belches *Sound of motor scooter arriving, sharp squeaking of brakes*	(Page 50)
Cue 21	**Mariette** throws her other shoe *Sound of motor scooter starting up and roaring away*	(Page 52)
Cue 22	At the end of Scene 1 *Cut television sound*	(Page 54)
Cue 23	**Lady Bluff-Gore**: "... so quiet." *Terrific bang from house; closely followed by other explosions from all around*	(Page 63)
Cue 24	**Angela Snow** throws a firework *Loud explosion*	(Page 64)
Cue 25	**Miss Pilchester** and **Pop** go off stage *Explosion, followed by more explosions all around*	(Page 64)
Cue 26	**Mariette**: "Pop, listen, listen, listen, listen." *More explosions*	(Page 64)
Cue 27	The twins and **Miss Pilchester** disappear into the house *Loud bang*	(Page 64)

CPSIA information can be obtained
at www.ICGtesting.com
Printed in the USA
LVHW040942281122
733859LV00018B/1860